FUROUT

SEMI-COZY PARANORMAL FUN

RENEE GEORGE

BARKSIDE OF THE MOON PRESS

FurOut: Witchin' Impossible Cozy Mysteries Book 5

Copyright © 2024 by Renee George

ISBN Print: 978-1-947177-52-9

Publisher: Barkside of the Moon Press

For my sister Robbin.
You are always there for me.
You are the best, my darling,
even when I'm bratty.
And for the other awesome Robyn in my life,
You are a miracle in friendship.
Thank you for all you do and are.

ACKNOWLEDGMENTS

Also, I must thank the usual suspects, my BFF sister and most fabulous beta reader Robbin, my BFF, and critique partner Robyn Peterman. You guys are like the chocolate to my almonds, the butter to my toast, and the sweetener to my tea. I love you like I love my left leg.

To my Rebels, you all RAWK! You keep me going every day with your support. I love you to the moon and back.

To my fans, I would not be anything without you. Seriously. If you keep reading, I'll keep writing! Thank you. Thank you. Thank you. If I were reviewing you all, you would get five-gazillion stars and a million-gazillion smooches.

Oh! And lest I forget, thank you strong, black coffee. Without you, I couldn't get out of bed in the morning, let alone write a single word.

Familiar allies. Old magic. New enemies. And a challenge to the death. In Paradise Falls, things have never been hairier.

In Paradise Falls, I'm the law. Since I became the police chief, crime here is about as common as a good hair day in a tornado, and peace between shifters and witches has never been smoother. My familiar, Tizzy the squirrel, keeps me entertained with her acorn-fueled antics, while my bear shifter hubby, Ford, makes me feel like the safest witch on the planet.

I should've known bliss never lasts. Like a vegan at a barbecue, trouble rolls into town in the form of a pack of werewolves. These furry interlopers aren't here for the scenic hikes or the artisanal honey—oh no, they want a piece of Paradise Falls, and they're not asking politely. When the Witch-Shifter Coalition votes to boot the wolves, the head howler throws down the gauntlet, declaring the sacred *Rite of Arphlitian*—a ritual fight to the death as ancient as the town's oldest oak tree.

With no choice, the town must choose a champion. And guess who volunteers? Yep, my honey-bear, Ford. As the new mayor, Ford steps up to the challenge, determined to defend our home.

I'm sure someone in town is conspiring with the newcomers to take down the leadership in Paradise Falls. But who? And to what end?

Unfortunately, in Paradise Falls, the only thing more magical than the town's charms is this mystery.

CHAPTER 1

THE MORNING SUN streamed through the window as I settled into my worn leather chair in my cluttered office. A harsh ray of light crossed my desk, drawing attention to the doom piles of paperwork I'd been avoiding all week. My coffee, a strong brew with a pinch of cinnamon, sat steaming beside a half-eaten donut.

Being Chief meant paperwork, people management, and politics. I'd scheduled a little one-on-one with the new mayor to discuss the police budget. The new guy was handsome and sexy, and it would be the highlight of my day. I looked at the time. Ten in the morning. Ugh. My meeting wasn't until two. Four long, tedious hours away.

The dispatch radio in my office was on for background noise. This morning there had been reports of a fender bender on Main Street, a noise complaint from Mrs. O'Malley's familiar again, and Officer Daniels managing traffic near the high school. Mundane, everyday police work in a town that had, in the past, been fraught with horrific murders, shifter-witch conflicts, a gaping tar pit to hell in the middle of Main Street, and enemies from the past rearing their ugly, revengeful heads. It was shaping up to be a typical morning in Paradise Falls.

In other words, I was bored out of my gourd.

I sighed heavily. "What I wouldn't give for a minor dustup. Nothing too catastrophic, but enough to get me out of this office for a few hours."

There is an old adage that goes, "Be careful what you wish for." It's an adage for a reason.

Our newest rookie officer, Becksy "Bex" Ansel, ran into my office. "Chief Kinsey, you need to hear this." The other officers started calling her Bex, rationalizing that Becksy was too cutesy of a name for a tough cop. I had full confidence in the young witch. Her skills as a police officer were as impressive as her magic.

"What's up?" I responded, eager for something mildly interesting to break up the morning.

Her perky nose twitched. "There's trouble out at the Junkyard Dog."

Junkyard Dog, an ironic name since the last owner Clayton Driver had been a cat shifter, was down a rough gravel road on the Merry County line.

The location also made it a perfect spot for criminal activity. Half the property was on Lister, the county that bordered ours, which made it a nightmare for law enforcement, considering jurisdiction was always in question. Still, it had been closed and unoccupied for eight years. Ever since Driver met his maker after trying to kill my best friend, the property had been about as lively as a sloth on vacation.

Less eagerly, I asked, "What kind of trouble?"

"Detective Edger called in on a private channel. He says there is a large group of unknown and dangerous-looking shifters with what looks like moving trucks heading to the Junkyard Dog," Bex answered, looking flustered.

I frowned. Patrick Edger, a weremongoose I had appointed the head of special investigations, had his nose and ears to the ground in Paradise Falls. If he said the group was unknown and dangerous, I believed him.

I got up and moved to the front of my desk. "Not good." Newcomers to Paradise Falls were rare, and anyone showing up without an invitation was immediately suspicious.

"He wants to know how you want him to handle the situation," Bex said.

My first impulse was to send a patrol car to investigate the strangers, but shifters could be unpredictable when challenged, even when you knew them well. I wouldn't send any of my officers into the potentially volatile situation until I had more information.

"Let's hold off on doing anything for a minute. Ask Patrick to observe from a distance. No direct contact with the strangers," I instructed. "I need to make a call."

She nodded and hurried back to her desk. I picked up my cell phone and dialed the mayor's number. He answered on the second ring.

"Hey, hot stuff." The newly appointed mayor, who also happened to be my dear husband, Ford Baylor, said in a low and seductive voice. "What're you wearing?"

I grinned at my mate's welcome audacity. "A nine-millimeter."

"Mmm," he growled. "And nothing else?"

I choked on a laugh. "As much as I want to finish this conversation," I replied, "and I do plan to finish it later, we've got a situation at the Junkyard Dog, and since my best officer up and quit on me..."

"I didn't just quit, Haze," he said gently,

"I know," I conceded. "I just miss having you around all the time." Being mated was more than just a signature on a piece of paper. It meant I always wanted to be wherever he was, holding on and loving him for the rest of our lives. Since Ford was a shifter, the feelings were even more intense for him.

"I miss you too." His tone was tender and reassuring. "Tell me about this situation. What's been reported?"

I sighed. Back to the business of business. "There's a report of new shifters in town. A whole group of them, apparently." I kept my voice steady despite the anxiety gnawing at me.

"New shifters?" Ford's surprise was palpable. "This is the first I'm hearing of it. They should've petitioned the coalition for an invitation before entering town. What are they up to?"

"That's what I'd like to know," I told him. "Patrick Edger says they have moving trucks. It makes me think they plan to stick around. Whatever their intent, they're trespassing on property that has been abandoned for a long time, making me even more nervous. Who owns the Junkyard Dog now?"

"I'll call down to records and find out whose name is on the deed." Ford was silent momentarily, and I could almost hear the gears turning in his mind. "Haze, we need to approach this carefully. I don't want a confrontation without knowing more about them."

"I agree. But we need to find out who they are and why they're here." My witchy senses were tingling. "I have a bad feeling about this."

"I do, too," he agreed. "But let's not rush into anything. I'll call a meeting with the Witch-Shifter

Coalition. Maybe someone knows something about these new arrivals. In the meantime, I want you to hold off on approaching them directly. Let's see if we can gather some information first."

"Maybe," I agreed reluctantly. "But we can't just sit back and do nothing."

"I know," Ford said. "We need to play this smart and safe."

"Understood," I said, feeling itchy. "If they're playing by shifter rules, they'll be expecting someone to show up and ask questions."

"If they were playing by shifter rules, they wouldn't have shown up unannounced," he countered.

"True." Still, I couldn't let the incursion into our town go unanswered. "I'll be the picture of diplomacy."

"Uh-huh," Ford said, unconvinced. "Don't go alone. Take a few of your witch officers as backup. Leave the shifters far enough away that the inter-lopers don't see it as a challenge."

I nodded even though he couldn't see me. "Good tip."

I could hear the rasp of his breath for a few seconds before he added, "Just promise you'll be careful."

"You got it," I assured him. "Let me know as

soon as you find anything out, and I'll keep you updated on my end."

"Check in often," Ford said, his voice softening.

I looked out the window at our sleepy town and across the street at the three-story courthouse. The building's dark, rough stone walls were centered by a tall square tower. When I was a kid, I always thought the arched windows framed by thick, carved columns made the building seem spooky. But since my sweetie became the big hunky-mucky-muck, I'd started seeing the beauty in the old building.

A small smile tugged at my lips when I saw Ford in his second-story office looking out of his window at me.

I waved at him. "I promise to check in."

He placed his large palm on the window. "I love you."

Like a double-barrel shotgun, my heart double-pumped. Our mate bond was locked and loaded. "I love you, too." After the call ended, I slipped my phone back into my pocket. When I turned around, I let out a little yip, sparks of magic shooting from my fingertips.

Sitting atop one of the paperwork piles, a large red, flying squirrel cracked an acorn as she stared at me.

"Don't sneak up on me."

"I've been here for like two minutes," she

informed me, her voice high and feminine. "I can't help it if you got the observational skills of a blind mole."

"I haven't been on the phone for two minutes."

"You've been moon-eyed staring across the road at Fozzie Bear since I popped in," she begged to differ. "You know you're time blind where that man is involved."

She wasn't wrong. It was one of the many reasons he decided to run for mayor. Since our wedding, neither of us was worth a damn at our jobs when the other was around. I raised a brow at my uninvited visitor. "Don't you have a restaurant to run? Won't Lupita be short-handed without you?"

Lupita, a pearl-gray Persian familiar that Tizzy had fallen in love with, had inherited her ex-witch Romy Quinn's restaurant after Romy went to jail for dabbling in dark magic and nearly destroying the whole town. Lupita was now my dad's familiar, but she and Tizzy had their own tiny house together on my property. Ford and I had a few acres surrounding our Victorian home, and setting up a tiny house so we could all have some needed privacy was a small sacrifice.

"Lupita has it handled."

"I have a lot going on today, Tiz. Tell me what you need and make it quick."

"I need you to tell me what you're going to do

about the pack of werewolves setting up territory in our area."

I narrowed my gaze at her. "Werewolves? What makes you think they're wolves? Or a pack?"

"I dated a pack bitch once," she said. "When they group like that, they take on a distinct scent."

"Mitzy Thomas is a wolf shifter, and she's great," I said.

"Mitzy is a *lone* wolf," Tizzy countered. "Besides, she was adopted and raised by cougar shifter parents, so it's not the same thing." Her whiskers fluttered as she sniffed. "When werewolves are in a pack, they're real jerks. They try to run everything. Trust me when I say you don't want their kind here."

"When did you date a wolf shifter?" I asked. "That seems like something I would've remembered. And how in the world? Logistically, it seems like a sizing nightmare."

"I've been around longer than you, Haze," she chittered. "I had a life before you. Several of them." She gave me a withering stare. "And I haven't always had this form, not that it's any of your business."

I put up my hands. "Fair enough." I often forgot that my familiar had a long, long history. It was easy to assume that she came into existence at the same time as I had, but that's not how it worked for her kind.

I gave her a go-ahead nod. "Okay, Ms. Werewolf

Pack Expert, if you had to take a guess as to why they're here, what would it be?"

She shrugged her tiny shoulders. "Secret shifterology cult? New age yoga retreat? Alien invasion?"

I chuckled. "Let's hope it's not aliens, Tiz. I don't want to have to explain to the coalition why crop circles are showing up in town."

"Whatever the reason, it's for sure going to be terrible," she quipped ominously.

It made me wonder just how badly her werewolf girlfriend had jilted her. It was a story for another time. Right now, I had a pack to check out.

"Bex!" I hollered. The young witch, work boots thudding against the linoleum floor, came running into my office.

"What's the plan, Chief?"

"I need every available witch officer to meet us at the Junkyard Dog."

"Us?" Bex asked. "As in you and me?"

"Yes, us," I told her. "I could use a strong witch in the field, and it will be good experience."

Bex hadn't been assigned a patrol partner yet, but I thought the girl had the makings of a good detective. Her years as a waitress at Lolo's Diner had given Bex a keen insight into shifters and witches and what motivated their behavior, whether it was food or crime.

Her back straightened. I could see she was pleased. "Got it, Chief. I'll radio all available units."

"Witches only," I reiterated. "We're going to see werewolves, and I don't want anyone accidentally starting a war."

She clicked her heels together, her arms rigid at her sides as she pivoted and raced back down the hall.

"Goddess in a pair of orange Uggs," Tizzy hissed. "For a minute, I thought she was going to salute."

"Leave the poor girl alone. She's excited."

"So was the Donner party when it started snowing," Tiz said.

I didn't love the picture the squirrel was painting. "We're not really worried about cannibalism, right??"

"Is it cannibalism when shifters eat you? Or do werewolves just call that dinner?"

"Don't invite them to a barbecue. Got it." I took my weapon from my office gun safe. "

"Be careful," warned Tiz. "Whatever they want, it's not gonna be good."

With those ominous words ringing in my ears, I strapped on my gun and left the office.

CHAPTER 2

WE PULLED up to the Junkyard Dog, just me and my witches. Seven of them, to be exact, counting Bex, who'd ridden shotgun with me. Some of my shifter officers had grumbled about waiting out of scenting distance, but the smart ones had known it was the right play. These newcomers weren't just any shifters. They were werewolves and total strangers. Both were things that we rarely if ever encountered in Paradise Falls. Other than the occasional human guest, our people had no experiences with any being or creature not native to our little town. The anxiety rolling off my officers as we parked and exited our vehicles was palpable.

"What do you think they'll be like?" Bex whispered as we walked toward the group of shifters carrying boxes into the junkyard's garage—a large building about half the size of a basketball court.

"I guess we're going to find out," I told her. I'd called Mitzy Taylor on her private line and asked if she had any insight into pack mentality. She'd nervously told me she hadn't a clue. Her parents had adopted her as an infant, and she'd never met any other wolf shifters.

The strong scent of dust and rust made my skin itch. Even in broad daylight, the place, with all the vehicle skeletons stacked up like bodies after a battle, gave me the creeps. There was a dilapidated trailer with a sign that read "management" on the front. I remembered the first time I'd come out here during my investigation of Danny Mason's death. I shivered as I remembered the gruesome nature of his demise. Clayton Driver, the previous owner of the place, had been part of a cabal of witches and shifters practicing dark druidic magic. The practice had required the extreme torture of shifters to generate the power they'd craved.

"That's a couch," Tiz said excitedly. The squirrel crawled up onto my shoulder, her nails clicking nervously. "This isn't a brief visit. I think they're moving into the neighborhood."

I watched as two men carried a plush brown English roll-arm sofa inside the office trailer. I reached up and stroked Tiz's tail. "Let's introduce them to the neighborhood watch... or rather, witch,"

I deadpanned, earning a quick snort of laughter from my furry companion.

"Should we... intervene?" Bex asked, glancing at me with an excited glint in her eyes. Her magic shimmered over her skin as she readied herself for trouble.

I prayed it didn't come to that. "Tamp that back and follow my lead," I cautioned. "We don't want to start anything we can't finish."

I considered the scene before us—shifters bustling about, clearly up to something mundane yet mysterious. The fact that they had found their way to Paradise Falls without an invitation was deeply suspicious. Even more suspicious, they weren't paying us any attention as they went about their work.

With a nod to Bex, I said, "Let's go find out who they are and why they've shown up in our quiet little town."

We approached the gang, their movements slowing as we got closer.

A tall man with a scar across his cheek, stepped out of the office trailer. His upper torso was muscled like a bodybuilder, jacked for power, and his lower half was lean and narrow as if built for speed.

His predatory gaze fixed on mine. "Morning, officers," he said, his voice a gravelly drawl. "Something we can help you with?"

"Morning," I replied evenly. "I'm Chief Hazel Kinsey, and we're not here to cause any problems. Just curious about what brings you folks to Paradise Falls. It's not exactly a place you stumble upon."

He smirked, eyes glinting with a mix of challenge and amusement. "We're just looking for a fresh start. Thought this place could use some new faces."

"Funny," I said, my tone remaining calm. "Paradise Falls tends to keep to itself. And it usually only welcomes those who are invited."

His smirk widened. "Guess we're lucky we got the invite then."

Invited? If anyone in town invited them, they would've run it past the coalition first. Either Scarface was lying or one of our residents was in seriously deep crap.

Tizzy bristled on my shoulder, but I kept my cool. "Lucky indeed. Who invited you?" I asked casually.

"A benevolent benefactor," he answered, nonplussed. "Anonymous."

I arched a brow at him. "Do you have a lease or something like it, permitting you to move onto this property?"

His grin widened, and I heard several of the other werewolves chuckle.

"Absolutely," he told me. He reached behind his back.

Several sparks from Bex's fingertips danced on the ground as my witches went on high alert.

I put my hand on her arm. "It's okay," I assured her, loud enough for the other officers to hear, as I kept my eyes on the scarred werewolf. "Go slow," I ordered him. "Don't want anyone getting spooked."

He laughed and held up his hands. "No need to get excited." He slowly turned around to show me his backside. "Just reaching for the deed. It's proof we have a right to be here." A sheath of white paper was folded and tucked into his back pocket. He patted the air at his crew as if to calm them. He reached back and, with two fingers, withdrew the folded paper from his jeans. He turned around, hands back in the air, before extending the hand with paperwork out toward me. "Here you go, Chief."

As I approached him, I noticed the other were-wolves had moved closer to their leader. The transition had been so subtle that I doubted anyone else had seen it. I reached out and took the offered paper. Unfolding it, I had to tamp down my shock and quickening pulse. The deed listed Brahmic Carvell Jensen as the owner of the junkyard and the surrounding twenty acres. The signature at the bottom, attesting to this, was Clayton Driver. But how? Had Driver sold his property before his death? And how in the world would he have even known this Jensen fellow?

I turned back to the leader, watching me with a knowing smirk. "Everything in order, Chief?"

"You Brahmic Carvell Jensen?"

"Yep," he quipped. "That would be me. My friends and family call me Brahm."

"Good to know, Mr. Jensen." I wasn't buying the folksy "aww-shucks" act. Neither was my familiar.

"Where's a good woodcutter when you need him," Tizzy tittered. I reached up to shush my petulant familiar.

"Don't worry, Little Red Riding Squirrel," he said to my familiar. "I won't be eating anyone today."

"Just today?" Bex asked.

He sized her up and down, then fixed her with an intense stare that made my rookie officer shrink and avert her eyes.

I wasn't a shifter, but my hackles rose. My instinct was to order my witches back to a safe distance, but our retreat would send the message— we were prey.

"Let's cut the big, bad wolf act." I narrowed my gaze at him. "What brings a bunch of werewolves to Paradise Falls?"

His smirk faded slightly, replaced by a more guarded expression. "We're just looking for a place to settle down. There's no crime in that."

"In a town like this, uninvited guests tend to raise eyebrows," I replied flatly. "Especially when they're werewolves. So, I'll ask again—why here, and why now?"

"We've got our reasons." Jensen widened his arms and spread his hands. "But don't worry, Chief. It's nothing for you and your witches to worry your pretty little heads about."

I gave him a slight nod. "If it's all the same to you, my pretty little head will worry about whatever I want."

He shrugged and scratched his five o'clock shadow. "Suit yourself."

Reluctantly, I handed him back the deed. "How did you know Clayton Driver?"

He glanced down briefly, then said, "Old hunting buddy."

I didn't need my best friend Lily Mason's ability to sniff out a lie to know this guy wasn't telling the truth.

"I promise you," Jensen said. "I'm not here to cause trouble."

"That remains to be seen," I said, meeting his gaze steadily. "In the meantime, you need to petition the Witch-Shifter Coalition if you plan to do any business in town." I dug one of the Coalition's cards out of my pocket. "Call to set up an appointment."

"Fair enough," he said, taking the card and holding out his other hand.

I wasn't prepared for war yet, so I shook the

offered hand, noting his firm grip. He let go and then nodded to his men to get back to work. Automatically, they started unloading the trucks again.

"Nice to meet you, Chief." Jensen's faint smile didn't reach his eyes. "We'll try to keep out of your hair."

"You do that," I told him.

I returned to the patrol car, Tizzy still bristling on my shoulder. The encounter hadn't given me any insight into the newcomers other than the fact that they were playing their cards close to their vests. As we drove away, I couldn't shake the feeling that this was just the beginning of something much bigger—and potentially far more dangerous. Paradise Falls had always been a haven for the supernatural, a place where different species coexisted in relative peace. The arrival of a werewolf pack threatened to disrupt that balance, and, unfortunately, it was up to me to ensure our town remained safe.

At least I had a name. That was a place to start. I picked up the phone and dialed a number I hadn't called in years. After a few rings, a familiar voice answered.

"Agent Sarah Hayes," came the crisp reply.

Sarah was my bunkmate at Quantico, and we'd stayed friendly until I left the FBI and moved back to Paradise Falls.

"Hey, Sarah. It's Hazel Kinsey," I said, my voice steady. "I need a favor."

There was a pause on the other end before Hayes responded, "I can't say yes until I know what it is."

Sarah was a mundane human and had no idea paranormal people like witches and shifters existed, so I knew I'd have to play it close to the vest. "I have a name I'd like a background check on."

"What has this name done?"

"Nothing yet," I assured her on a chuckle. "Want to keep it that way."

There was another brief pause before she said, "Fine. Give me the name, but you owe me a bottom-less margarita at La Hacienda."

"Deal," I told her. "Brahmic Carvell Jensen."

"Got it," she said. "I'll see if there's anything to dig up."

"Thanks, Sarah." I had a thought. "See if his name comes up in conjunction with a Clayton Driver."

"Elroy," Bex said from the passenger seat. "His middle name is Elroy."

"Heard," Sarah said efficiently. "Will check out Jensen and Driver. And Hazel, margaritas when this is over," she said with a hint of a smile in her voice. "Then you can tell me all about life as a local-yokel."

"That's Chief Local-yokel," I laughed.

"It's good to hear from you, Hazel."

I smiled. "It's good to be heard from."

"Talk soon," she finished, then disconnected the call.

As nice as it had been to hear Sarah's voice, I couldn't shake the "hairy" ball of anxiety growing in the pit of my stomach. In Paradise Falls, nothing was ever simple, and the arrival of werewolves made it even more complicated. It was time to dig deeper, get our hands dirty, and find out what these strangers were really after before their presence turned our quiet little town into a battleground.

CHAPTER 3

ON MY WAY back to the station, I called Ford and let him know how my introduction to Brahm Jensen and his pack had gone. On his end, he told me Tyris Chestnut, the court clerk, was having difficulty locating the deed to Clayton Driver's property. That was no surprise. Each thing we discovered was shadier than the last.

I'd instructed Patrick to keep up surveillance on the Junkyard Dog and its occupants. Sitting behind a desk, with trouble brewing at the edge of our county, was hard. Unfortunately, there was nothing to be done about the werewolves until I had more information, or they did something stupid enough for me to have an excuse to run them out of town.

My cell phone rang as I poured myself a cup of steaming-hot liquid patience, known as coffee. I recognized the number immediately—Sarah Hayes.

It was the call I'd been waiting for, and I hoped to Hades she found something I could use against Jensen.

"That was quick," I answered, keeping my voice steady. "Find anything good?"

"Some," Sarah replied. "Not anything federal worthy, but he's got priors."

"Oh yeah?" I scooted forward in my seat and grabbed a pencil, ready to jot notes on my legal pad. "Let me have it."

"Well, your boy Brahmic Carvell Jensen's rap sheet consists mostly of assaults, bar fights, that sort of thing. No major felonies on his record, but there's a pattern that caught my eye. Wherever he and his crew go, there's trouble. We're talking disappearances in small towns, unsolved crimes, you name it. Nothing that sticks to them, mind you, so I can't confirm he's responsible, but it would be a mighty coincidence if he weren't involved. He and his gang are ghosts—here one day, gone the next, leaving chaos in their wake."

I frowned, my fingers tightening around the phone. "Sounds like a party," I said flatly. Jensen might've been a wreck 'em and leave 'em guy in the past, but I had a sinking feeling he wasn't planning on leaving Paradise Falls. At least not anytime soon. He had a land deed in hand and was acting like a man who wanted to put down roots. "Got anything on his connection to Clayton Driver?"

"That's where it gets murky," Sarah replied, the sound of papers rustling in the background. "No mention of Driver, but there's a vague mention of some secret society—something old and powerful. Just rumors and whispers, like he was part of something bigger, something dark."

The information was troubling, to say the least. My mind raced with possibilities, none of them good. "Where did the rumor originate?"

"From a witness to one of the disappearances."

"Still in play?"

"Dead, I'm afraid." She paused for a moment. "This is going to sound nuts, but he was mauled by an animal at Mammoth Spring State Park in Arkansas. Critter unknown."

"You're right," I told her. "Sounds nuts." I shook my head. More than likely, the witness ran into a vicious werewolf, but I couldn't exactly say that to Sarah.

"Hey, if you find evidence on this guy, loop me in. I'd love to pin some federal charges on his elusive ass."

"Sure thing." Even as I said it, I knew I was lying. I wasn't planning on "looping" her in on anything. Shifters doing human jail time wasn't a good idea. No. If I found any evidence of wrongdoing, Jensen would see justice played out paranormal-style. "Thanks for the call back and the info, Sarah. I owe you one."

"More like two," she countered, a hint of a smile returning to her voice. "And don't forget that bottomless margarita."

"Wouldn't dream of it," I said, though my heart wasn't in it.

After we ended the call, I leaned back in my chair, staring at the ceiling as I processed the information. Brahm Jensen wasn't just some drifter looking for a fresh start—he was a potential threat and a serious one at that. His connection to a secret society had my instincts on high alert. The last secret society this town saw had involved Clayton Driver, and it nearly destroyed Paradise Falls.

"Knucker's knockers, Haze." Tizzy hopped onto my desk and perched on a doom pile. "You look like you've seen a hellhound."

Knucker's were sea serpents. Not real, as far as I knew. Hellhounds? That was another story. Seeing them meant someone you loved would die. I hadn't run into a hellhound before, and I hoped to never. "Go home, Tiz." I was tired and didn't have the mental or emotional capacity to exchange banter.

Tizzy didn't move. Instead, she leveled her dark brown gaze on me. "I heard you on the phone." She started sharpening her sparkly silver claws. "What did your feebie friend say?"

"What we already knew." I scrubbed my face with my palms. "He's a bad dude."

"I could've saved you a phone call if that's all you got. I could sniff that the dude was bad news from a mile away."

I studied my eon's old familiar for a moment.

"Do I have a booger on my face?" she asked, swiping at her nose.

"No." I cracked a smile. I couldn't help it. Tizzy was adorable and it was hard to be somber around her. "My contact said that Jensen might belong to some secret and powerful society."

My squirrel familiar hissed. "You mean like the Arete."

I nodded solemnly. The Arete had been a society of witches and shifters in our county who had gone to great lengths to take power through dark, druidic magic. Clayton Driver had been a member. Was Jensen an Arete as well? The thought made me shiver. The group had perpetrated pure evil. I would never get the image of Boyd Decker's mangled and bloated body out of my head. Driver and his cronies had turned the harmless raccoon shifter into something unrecognizable and left his remains for his parents to find. Like I said, pure vicious evil.

"This is going to get nasty," Tiz stated the obvious. "And not in a fun way."

My phone rang. It was Ford, so I picked it up before the second ring. "Hey, I'm glad you called. My FBI contact called me back. Jensen is a troublemaker, but nothing ever sticks to him. I'm worried we're heading for a world of hurt."

I could hear Ford's heavy sigh. "I'm afraid my news isn't good either. Driver's land deed records and all records related to the man are gone. Disappeared. We've got nothing to counter what Jensen showed you."

"An inside job?" I asked.

"I can only assume," he answered. "Jensen called the coalition after you left him. He's got a meeting with them at three-thirty. They want us there by three to brief them on what we know."

"Solid plan." If we wanted to get rid of the werewolf, we needed the coalition to back our play. "You want to swing by and pick me up or meet me there?"

The missing records made things even more unsettling. Either someone in our town was helping the werewolves with whatever they had planned, or something much bigger was at play. The legal paperwork's disappearance only added to the growing unease that had taken up residence in my gut. I would have to coordinate with my officers to get eyeballs on the coalition office. I wanted them set up before Jensen arrived, just in case I needed backup.

"I'll meet you there," Ford said. "I have a meeting at two-forty-five with the housing committee. I've put it off twice and can't do it a third time."

"I'll see you there then."

"Love you," he said as a goodbye.

"Love you more." I hung up and pushed the intercom button on my phone. "Bex," I said. "I need all officers who aren't on patrol in the briefing room."

Her voice came over the speaker. "When?"

"Now."

"You got it, Chief," she quipped.

Tizzy chittered excitedly. "We're back, baby."

"This is going to get dangerous," I reminded her. "It's not a game."

"You're right," she said, not even a little abashed. "And it's a not-game that we're going to win."

CHAPTER 4

I PULLED onto Heavenly Street and parked in an empty spot in front of the DMV. The Witch-Shifter Coalition was next door, and all the choice spots were taken. The office was in a historical two-story brick building with lead glass windows and large wooden double doors. I walked past the empty front office and into the inner sanctum. Six ornately carved high-back chairs lined a stage-like area. Six people, two women and four men, were seated, all with the same look on their faces as my high school principal when she'd caught me smoking in the girl's room my junior year. I'll admit I found the idea of being suspended for three days appealing.

The witch side of the coalition consisted of my dad, Kent Kinsey, Golda Gedes, a local historian, and Tanya Gellar, the local doctor-slash-medical examiner. Tanya and I had a long, unpleasant history that went back to high school but we'd developed a grudging respect over the past few years. The fact that she was dating my dad had taken a hot minute to get used to, but I'd made my peace with their relationship, as well.

On the therianthrope side, we had bear shifter Bryant Baylor, my father-in-law and Arcturus for the bears and other large shifters in town. Next to him was cougar shifter Mary Lowe, matriarch for the *felidae*, and then raccoon shifter Steve Crandell, the *paullulum mammalia*, aka the tiny critters alpha.

"Where's Ford?" Bryant asked.

"He'll be here," I said. "He had a meeting he couldn't get out of."

"Bunch of bureaucratic B.S.," Steve complained. "This is more important than politics."

"Now, Steve," Mary soothed. "The boy has a town to run. He'll be here when he gets here."

I was sure Ford would love being called boy...not. Mary was older than his mother and had known him since he was in diapers, so I knew he'd give her a pass.

Steve piped up again. "I hope it's before Jensen shows." The small critter alpha looked as nervous as a chicken in a wolf's den. I couldn't blame him. His people were prey animals, and a whole pack of predators showing up didn't bode well for them.

"Ford will be along shortly," I promised, hoping it

wasn't a lie. Brahm Jensen had looked at me in a way that made my skin crawl. I'd feel better having my mate by my side when he and his werewolves arrived, too.

"Me too, but while we're waiting, I'll fill you all in on what I know so far. I ended by summarizing Sarah's findings, leaving nothing out. "I'm worried about what his affiliation with Clayton Driver means." The room was silent as I spoke, the gravity of the situation sinking in.

Tizzy perched on my shoulder, her tail twitching. "The coalition is wound tighter than a hydra's butt-hole after bad sushi."

The visual gave me the ick. "Thanks for that," I said. "You should've been a comedienne."

She puffed her chest out. "I'm here all week, and I perform for nuts."

"You are nuts." I scanned the silent coalition, worried that I'd broken their brains. "Do you want me to go over it again?"

"Not necessary, dear," Mary Lowe replied. "We're just taking a moment to digest the information. If I understand correctly, you're worried you didn't iden-tify all of Adele's followers. You're worried there's someone in town that is still a part of her cult."

"Correct." I nodded. Adele Adams had been the witch behind most of the Arete's activities in town. As far as I knew, the main players had been her,

Clayton Driver, Robert Townsend, and Frank Leggert. Townsend, the old little critter alpha, had been a coalition board member like Adele. On the other hand, Frank had been just a beaver shifter who enjoyed his booze and had a mean streak. He'd gotten into a drunken fight with Tizzy after she kissed his wife at a party. All of them were dead now, so none of them could be responsible for bringing the wolves to town. "I'm worried that there's still someone who's following her teachings. Maybe more."

"More?" Tanya asked, horrified. "You mean there might be more than one person still on that crazy's train?"

"Give that lady a prize," Tizzy announced. "She's not as dumb as she looks."

Tanya narrowed her gaze on my squirrel. She reached out and took my father's hand. "Sweetheart," she said to him, flipping her wavy, strawberry-blonde hair with the back of her other hand. "How does squirrel and dumplings sound for dinner?"

My dad shook his head. "Lupita would never go for it."

"And neither would Hazel," Tizzy exclaimed. She looked at me. "Right, Haze?" When I didn't reply, she asked again, "Right, Haze?"

"Your mouth is going to get you barbecued," I replied. "But right."

She giggled. "Like I always say, if nobody's threatening to roast you over a spit, you're not trying hard enough."

I gave Tanya a nod. "To answer your question, yes, I believe the Arete is a larger group than we initially realized. If the new werewolves in town are affiliated with the Arete, then it's not merely a few rogue witches and shifters trying to seize power. It's a much more extensive network. One that could stretch across the country and possibly even the globe."

"Then we definitely don't want them getting a toehold in our area," Steve said.

My dad finally spoke up. "I thought this might be shifter business, but it sounds like Jensen's presence in our town is bad for everyone."

Steve stared at my dad. "Who's to say Kinsey isn't involved? If the rumors are true his wife had been part of Adele's group."

"And she's dead," Bryant interjected. "At Kent's hands. Which in my book puts him in the good guy territory."

I know my father-in-law was trying to help, but ouch. My dad hadn't killed my mother on purpose. After he'd discovered his wife had been responsible for the deaths of my BFF Lily's parents, my father had tried to sever the matrimony bond that tied the two of them together as husband and wife. The spell to break the soul-deep tie was tricky and dangerous on a good day and could've killed both my parents. As it was, only my mother had died. Dad had spent almost two decades in witch-prison for the crime.

Dad remained stoic, but I could see the accusation smarted. His eyes widened a hair as he took his phone from his pants, quickly checked the screen, and then put it back.

Ford walked in, and my shoulders sagged with relief. "Glad you could make it," I half-heartedly teased as he took his place beside me.

He glanced around the room, his expression determined. "I'm sure Hazel got you all up to speed."

Bryant nodded "Jensen will be here soon. He thinks he's going to get permission to stay in Paradise Falls, but we all know that's not going to happen. We need to make it clear that he and his pack need to leave."

There were murmurs of agreement from the other members of the coalition.

"And how are we going to do that?" Ford asked. "Hazel says his name is on the deed to the property, and I can't find any evidence to the contrary."

"Because someone got rid of all the paperwork," Tanya said. She straightened her back and then gestured in my direction. "Can't you do one of your reveal spells to find out who messed with the court records?"

My reveal spell didn't quite work like that, as Tanya well knew. She was the medical examiner in town and had worked on a few cases with me. Even so, a reveal spell wasn't a bad idea. "I can try and see what I can see." I shrugged. "The spell can't give me the who, but it might point me in the right direction."

"Hush," my father cautioned us. "Jensen has arrived."

I hadn't heard anything. Had my father developed super hearing? "How do you know?"

He slipped a phone from his pocket and showed me the screen. "New security cameras outside the building. It sends an alert anytime someone opens the front door."

That must have been why he'd been checking it before Ford arrived. The door swung open, and Brahm Jensen strode into the room. As he entered, two of his pack members flanked him, and the tension in the room was thick enough to cut with an athame.

"Well, well. The gangs all here." He winked at me. "Looks like I'm right on time," Brahm said smoothly, his gaze sweeping over the gathered council members before landing on me again. His leering grin made my stomach knot. He turned back to the seated coalition members. "It's a pleasure to greet you," he said, oddly formal. "The Wayward Impala Pack presents itself in open friendship and kinship." His two sidekicks snickered. He gave them a withering stare, and they immediately sobered. "Excuse my second and my beta." Jensen's eyes were hard. "They've forgotten their manners. It's been a while since we've had to ask permission to be somewhere."

"I bet his sidekicks think 'manners' is a new deodorant." Tizzy waved her hand in front of her nose. "So they avoid it like the stinkers they are."

The tug of a smile on the alpha werewolf's lip and the bristling of his cronies told me they'd heard her.

I reached up and patted her tail to quiet her.

Jensen gestured to one of his men, a guy with shoulder-length, dishwater blond hair. He was nearly as big as Brahm in size and height. "This is Ardell, my second." The other man had dark brown hair and was stockier but shorter by several inches than them. "And this is Richard, my beta."

"Great," Tiz muttered. "All this town needs is another Dick."

This time I gave her tail a yank.

"Ow," she complained. "That hurt."

"They can hear you," I whispered.

"I know," she whispered back. "That's the point."

Brahmic Jensen's gaze was steely for a moment before he barked a laugh. "Squirrel's got a point. Richard has always been a bit of a dick."

The shorter man snarled, staring murderous daggers in Tiz's direction.

"Anyhow," Jensen said. "Now that we've had our introduction, we'll be on our way home."

"That's not how this works," Steve said. "You need our permission to stay."

"Oh." Jensen shook his head. "Are you saying you're not planning on giving it?"

The raccoon shifter visibly recoiled.

"That's exactly what he's saying." Bryant rose to his feet, showing solidarity with his coalition counterpart. "You need our permission." Brahm Jensen was big, but the bear shifter was even bigger. Bryant's deep voice was edged with anger, and his normally calm demeanor was fraying. "We don't want you here, and we certainly don't want you disrupting our town."

"Too bad, so glad I'm not you because I'm not going anywhere," Jensen snarled. "My pack and I have every right to be here." He held up the document he'd shown me earlier. "This meeting is a mere formality." He waved his free hand in a flourish. "A courtesy, if you will. But don't think for a moment that I'll vacate my legal and rightful property because you all have your panties in a twist."

"That's not up to you," Bryant said. "Paradise Falls has its own set of rules. I'm Arcturus. Which means there's no place for you or your pack here."

Brahm's smile didn't waver, but there was a glint of something dangerous in his eyes. "That's disappointing to hear, Arcturus, but I suspected as much. Which is why I'm invoking the *Rite of Arphlitian*."

A heavy silence fell over the room. My stomach twisted as I glanced at Ford, who appeared more than a little surprised by Jensen's declaration—he looked worried. I'd never heard of the rite before, but it didn't take a rocket scientist to know it wasn't a good thing.

"What's the *Rite of Arphlitian*?" I asked, my voice cutting through the silence. I turned to Ford, hoping for an explanation.

He exchanged a grave look with Bryant, then said, "It's an ancient shifter tradition, Hazel. A duel to the death, used to settle territorial disputes. The winner claims the territory for themselves, and the loser... well, they don't survive."

"A duel? To the death?" My blood ran cold as I pivoted my gaze to Jensen. "No." I clenched my fists, ready to throat punch the bastard. "It's a resounding unequivocal, not-only-no-but-hell-no no."

"The Rite can't be refused," Jensen said, a smug smile spreading across his face.

I gave Ford a pleading stare. I needed him to back me up on this.

Instead, he reluctantly met my gaze then shook his head. "It can't be refused."

My father-in-law fighting someone to the death hadn't been on my list of things that might happen today. I scanned the coalition members, hoping someone sane would pipe up. I gestured at them. "Someone make this make sense."

Golda Gedes, our historian, gave it a go. "The *Rite of Arphilitian* is an ancient and acknowledged ritual that allows shifters to settle territorial disputes. Dating back as far as recorded history can go, it's been crucial for their identity and survival. This rite is performed during special lunar phases or celestial events. Two challengers face off, under strict rules to ensure fairness. No shifting, no magic, and no interference. The winner gains control of the disputed territory." Her expression was sad as she cast a glance at Bryant. "As Mayor Bryant said, the rite can't be ignored. It's deeply embedded in shifter culture and spirituality. Ignoring it would disrupt their societal structure and invite divine retribution, as it's seen as both a spiritual and cultural necessity to maintain order and prevent chaos."

Prevent chaos? Too freaking late. Chaos was not

only on the menu, it was the freaking special of the day.

Brahm's smile widened, clearly enjoying the reaction his challenge had provoked. "Exactly. And since your council seems so adamant about not granting my pack the sanctuary we need, I think it's only fair to settle this matter in the old ways."

Bryant Baylor was already stepping forward, his eyes blazing with fury, but Ford stopped him with a hand on his arm. "No, Dad," Ford said, his voice quiet but firm. "I'm the one who has to do this."

A soft noise of protest escaped me.

Bryant shook his head. "I'm the Arcturus. It's my responsibility—"

Ford's expression was earnest. "I'm your second, and as such, I can be your champion." He gave his dad a reassuring nod. "I'm also the mayor of this town, so that sort of puts me at the top of the food chain over the witches and the shifters. It's my job to take on any territory disputes because it will affect not only the shifters under you but the witches and shifters under the rest of the coalition."

Mary said, "I accept Ford as my champion."

Steve followed suit. "I accept Ford as my champion."

I blinked back tears, filled with disbelief at what I was hearing. Then my dad, Tanya, and Golda all accepted Ford as well. Bryant was the only hold out.

Ford put his hand on Bryant's shoulder. "Dad? Will you accept me as your champion?"

Bryant bristled with anger and anxiety. Finally, he said, "Your mother's going to kill me."

Ford arched a brow at his father, the barest hint of a smile on his lips. "Is that a yes?"

The tension in the room was nearly unbearable as Bryant stepped back, his jaw clenched tight with the effort. He nodded. "Yes, that's a yes, my son. I accept you as my champion."

It took every ounce of courage and willpower not to cry out. Now wasn't the time to argue with Ford. The damage was done, but boy-howdy, the man was going to get an earful as soon as we were alone.

Ford turned to face Jensen, his expression hardening into one of resolve. "I accept your challenge. In two days' time, we will fight when the perigee moon rises," he said, his voice steady. "But know this, I will do whatever it takes to protect this town. Paradise Falls will never belong to you."

Jensen's eyes glittered with satisfaction. "We'll see about that." Without another word to us, Brahm and his pack strode out of the meeting. I heard Dick ask, "What's a perigee moon?" Then he squawked when Jensen cuffed him in the back of the head as they went out the front door. It felt like the temperature had dropped several degrees, the chill settling deep into my bones.

"It's a supermoon," Tizzy said quietly. "In case you were wondering."

I wasn't. As chief, I had to be aware of all the full moons, because shifter crime went up significantly during them. I stared at Ford, my heart pounding with fear and rage. The determination in his eyes, the resolve in his voice—it should have reassured me, but it didn't. Instead, I felt like I was watching him walk straight into the lion's den.

But the fear that gripped me wasn't something I could shake off so easily. I could see Brahm's smirk in my mind, the cold calculation in his eyes. This wasn't a challenge to him—it was a game. A game he'd played before and one that had likely ended in the death of his opponent every time.

The rest of the Coalition members were watching us, their expressions a mix of concern and determination. My father stepped forward, his face etched with worry but also an abundance of respect.

"We'll do everything we can to support you, Ford," Kent said, his voice steady. "But this town can't afford to lose you."

"And we'll keep a close watch on the pack to make sure they don't try anything funny," Steve added, his gaze serious. "Cheating will be an instant forfeit."

"Thank you," Ford said. "I'll take all the help I can get."

As we left the Coalition building, I couldn't shake the gnawing dread in my gut. The werewolves had brought darkness with them, and that darkness was spreading, threatening to consume everything in its path. One thing was certain, though, Ford and I had much to discuss, and I was sure he wasn't going to like what I had to say. Brahm Jensen wasn't just a threat to the town—he was a threat to the man I loved. And no matter what, I wouldn't let him take Ford away from me.

CHAPTER 5

AS FORD and I drove to his parents' house, the sun had just slipped below the horizon, painting the late August sky in shades of salmon and tangerine. A large, nearly full moon took on an orange glow as it rode the coattails of the sunset. It was a harsh reminder of what was looming in two days.

I'd been silent for several blocks, trying to tamp down my fury at my husband and mate. He'd made a decision that affected both of us without even pausing to consider the consequences.

"Ford, what the hell were you thinking?" I demanded, my voice rough with emotion. I hadn't wanted to explode in front of the others, but now that we were alone, I let him have it with both barrels. "You know what this means, right? This isn't just some fight—you accepted a challenge to the death." I punched his shoulder as my fingers began sparking with barely contained magic. I hit him three more times. "To. The. Death."

He turned onto his parents' street, his expression a mix of calm and resolve that only made my anxiety spike.

"I know what it means, Hazel," he said quietly as he parked in front of their two-story home. Only then did he meet my furious gaze. "But I didn't have a choice. I couldn't let my dad take the challenge. He's strong, but he's never had to fight for his life. He inherited the role of Arcturus."

"I get that you didn't want your dad in harm's way, but seriously, I'm your wife. Your mate. We're bonded. If you die, our bond is severed. You remember what happened when my dad severed his bond?"

"Your mom..." His eyes widened. "I...I didn't think—"

I punched him again. "You sure didn't think!" I wasn't worried for myself, even if it sounded like it. I just wanted him to grasp the full weight of what he'd done by accepting that stupid challenge from Jensen.

"I'm sorry, love. It's too late to back out now. If I do, the town and all the shifters under our protection become Jensen's. He and his pack will take over this place, and then it'll be open season on anyone who stands in their way."

"He's a killer, Ford," I said, my voice shaking. "I

saw it in his eyes. This isn't the first time he's issued this kind of challenge, and I bet it's why people have disappeared in other towns he's passed through."

My husband's jaw tightened, but he didn't look away. "I know," he admitted, his voice low and steady. "But if I don't stop him here, those disappearances will continue. And it won't just be strangers. It'll be our people, Hazel—our friends, our families. I can't let that happen."

Fear twisted in my chest, sharp and painful. Ford was a bear shifter, and as a former deputy, he'd seen his share of violence. But he wasn't like Jensen. The thought of Ford facing someone like that, someone who lived by a ruthless code, filled me with dread.

"You're not like him," I said, my voice breaking. "You're not a stone-cold killer, Ford. You can't just—"

"I can handle Jensen," he interrupted, his voice firm. "I have to do this, Hazel. It's the only way to protect everyone."

If he lost, his sacrifice wouldn't mean much. Not to me or this town. Jensen would get exactly what he wanted, and the rest of us would be in deep trouble. Worse, I'd be without the love of my life, my reason for getting up every day, and the cause of my sleepless nights. I didn't want to live without him. A part of me hoped that if he didn't survive, I would die with him. I shook the thought from my head. I couldn't think about Ford failing. He had to win and live. We had a long, beautiful life ahead of us, and I'd be damned if some testosterone-fueled challenge was going to take that away.

As it was, his mind was made up. The look in his eyes told me that no amount of reasoning would change it. He wasn't just doing this because of his duty as mayor or some misplaced sense of honor. He was doing it because he loved his dad, this town, and its people.

But that didn't make it any easier to accept.

"We'll find a way to even the odds," I finally said, my voice trembling as I fought to keep my emotions in check. "There has to be something we can do, some way to make sure you—" I stopped, unable to say the words aloud.

"Survive?" Ford finished for me, his voice softening. He reached out, taking my hand in his warm and reassuring grip. "Cheating's not an option, but I'm not planning on losing, Hazel. When this is over, Jensen will be six feet under."

A knock at the window startled me. Anita Baylor's angry face stared daggers at her oldest son. Apparently, Bryant had filled her in on the news. Oh boy. Dinner was going to be a real blast.

"Come in, you two," she snapped. "Food's getting cold."

We got out of the truck and headed inside. The

smell of roasted chicken and herbs filled the air, and for a moment, I allowed myself to enjoy the comforting familiarity of it.

Bryant was standing near the buffet, his expression grim.

"Bryant told me about the new arrivals," Anita began, her voice heavy with concern. "A werewolf pack in Paradise Falls...And the challenge." Her hands balled into fists at her sides. "I'm ready to spit nails."

I recognized the pain behind her anger and knew it well.

"I know," I replied, meeting her gaze. "I'm right there with you."

Bryant's jaw tightened. "You shouldn't have usurped my right to accept the challenge."

Ford reached out and placed a hand on his father's arm. "It was the right thing to do, Dad. I know you want to protect Paradise Falls too, but I'm the town leader, not just the alpha of the largest shifter faction. It's my place to do it as a representative for all the shifters and witches under my leadership, not yours."

"I hate this," Anita said. "Why can't we just gather a group of our strongest people and evict the son-of-a-bee-sting? We have witches, which gives us the upper hand."

"You know the *Rite of Arphlition* is binding,"

Bryant told his wife. "Any interference to stop the challenge or change the outcome by cheating or using magic will forfeit our claim to this territory."

"And who would enforce this claim?" I asked.

"This from the woman whose grandmother is the Grand Inquisitor for all the witches?" Bryant, looking older than I'd ever seen him, gave me a baleful stare. "Just like the witches have an enforcement arm, so do the shifters. We have rules that must be followed, and if we break them, the consequences will be dire."

I glanced at Ford. "How come I've never heard of this arm of shifter law?"

"Because they rarely have to act, and we make sure we don't do anything in our little town to draw their attention."

"How would they even know about the challenge?"

"Because if Jensen has put it forward, it means he's already communicated his intent with the PEB."

"PEB?"

"Protean Enforcement Bureau." Ford sighed. "Their soldiers are called Beastwardens."

"Seriously?" The whole thing sounded like some real scary black ops. "Have you ever met anyone from this PEB? Or is it just a ghost story shifter parents tell their kids to keep them in bed at night?"

"I've met one before," Anita said in a hushed

tone. "We don't want them coming to Paradise Falls. Not for any reason."

Bryant walked over to his wife and put his arm around her shoulders. "Anita's father was removed by a Beastwarden when she was a cub."

"I thought you said they'd never been in Paradise Falls."

"I'm not from here originally," she told us.

That came as a shock to me. By the expression on Ford's face, this was the first he'd heard of it too.

"My family were homesteaders. Shifters who lived outside a human town. My dad farmed, and we raised livestock to sell at the market."

"Where?" Ford asked. "Where did you live?"

"Mid-Missouri, outside a town called LaMonte." Her eyes grew wistful. "It was one of those places that if you blinked too long while driving past it, you'd miss the whole thing."

"So not that different from here," I muttered.

Anita continued, "I was so young, but I still vividly remember the day the Beastwarden came and took him."

"What had he done?"

"He killed a werecoyote."

"For what?" Ford's tone was disbelieving. "Chasing chickens?"

She gave him a sharp, admonishing glare, then

shook her head. "He caught the shifter trying to rape a human one night when he was in town."

"Holy crap." My eyes widened. "It sounds like the guy had it coming."

"The coyote had been the alpha of his group. His second wanted our whole family dead as retribution for not issuing a formal challenge to their leader. It made the execution of the coyote a serious offense."

"But the guy was a rapist."

"The PEB don't care about humans. Shifter politics is their only concern." I could hear the anger behind her words. "My mother and I were lucky. The Beastwarden convinced the coyotes to leave us alone."

"And your dad?"

"We never saw him again." She took Bryant's hand. "I don't want anyone else in my family to disappear."

"Same." I nodded to Ford. "So, what can we do?"

Bryant took the seat at the head of the table. "We have to let it play out. There will be a supermoon in two days, and Ford will have to fight." He sighed, leaning back in his chair. "Until then, we have to keep the werewolves from doing anything stupid in town and inciting a riot."

"Agreed," I said, sitting down in my regular chair to the left of Bryant and next to Ford. I liked being near my mate, even if the table seemed lopsided with two of us on one side. Anita, who usually sat at the other end, took the chair opposite me next to her husband. I wasn't the only one who wanted to be near their mate.

I inhaled Ford's delicious cinnamon scent as he took the chair beside me. He scooted in until his stomach touched the edge of the table, and I slid my hand over his thigh. "We need to be smart about this. Any confrontations can be seen as interference. We can't afford that until after the rite."

We ate our meal in silence, but the tension lingered. When dessert arrived—fresh blackberry cobbler with vanilla ice cream—the tune "Bad Boys" blared from my phone. It was the ringtone I used when dispatch patched a call through to me.

"I'm so sorry," I told Anita, rising to retrieve my cell from my purse. With the werewolves in town, I couldn't afford to ignore it. "It's work." I answered the call. "What's going on?"

Mitzy Thomas responded, "Got a problem at Lolo's Diner, Chief. Some of Jensen's crew are riling up the regulars and acting like real jerks."

"Any fights?" I asked, hoping it would give me a reason to ban them from town.

"Not yet. You said the shifters had to keep a safe distance from the pack, so I'm checking in to see how you want us to handle the situation."

"Unless they break the law, leave them alone for

now. Hopefully, they'll be out of our hair for good in a couple of days." It occurred to me that Mitzy, a lone wolf in town, might be having a tougher time with the pack's sudden appearance. "Are you doing okay, Officer Thomas? I mean, with all this."

"I'm good, Chief. You don't have to worry about me." Her voice was throaty and tight, which made me worry more.

"Swap out with Newsome and Petry," I suggested.

"I'm good, Chief," she reiterated. "John and I have it under control."

Mitzy's partner John Parker was a warlock and her mate. I knew from personal experience how grounding it was to have your mate by your side. "Fine," I told her. "But call me back if they don't clear out soon."

Ford waved at me. "I'll call Beatrice and have her close Lolo's early tonight."

"I heard him, Chief," Mitzy said. "It's a temporary solution. And what if the werewolves refuse to leave?"

"Then call me," I repeated. "Don't try to handle it yourselves. Some things went down tonight that I'll explain tomorrow. I want every officer at the station at oh-nine-hundred for a briefing."

"Heard," she answered. "I'll keep you posted."

I disconnected the call. "I guess you all heard

that. I'm not sure we're going to make it to the supermoon without an incident."

"I wish I could disagree," Bryant said, his heavy brows furrowing. "If I thought it would solve the problem, I'd kill Jensen now and take my punishment."

"Bryant Clover Baylor, don't talk like that," Anita snapped. "I won't hear it."

"Sorry, dear," he said, looking abashed. "I didn't mean it."

"Ooooooo, you got told, Papa Bear," Tizzy said, suddenly appearing on the Baylors' dining table. She plucked a black olive from the salad and nodded to Anita. "What's cooking, Mama B?"

"Get off my table, Tiz, or it's going to be roast squirrel."

Tizzy's voice rose an octave. "Why is everyone talking about eating me today?"

"What are you doing here?" I asked my familiar. "Why aren't you home with Lupita?"

"Because I've been out scouting, Goldilocks."

At least she hadn't called me baby bear. I arched a brow at her. "Scouting what?"

"The werewolves are up to no good at the junkyard."

"What did you see?"

"It's not what I saw; it's what I felt." She rubbed her paws over her arms as if warding off goosebumps. "They're doing something inside the garage that feels downright evil."

"I'm surprised you didn't sneak a peek." That didn't sound like my nosy familiar at all. "Did they have it well guarded?"

"Yes, but that's not the problem, Haze." She threw up her hands. "The building has some kind of shielding. I couldn't get inside. It's totally poof-proof!"

"A magic shield?"

"That'd be my guess, but it doesn't feel like witchcraft."

"Fudge knuckles." Magic that wasn't witchcraft was further evidence that Jensen and his pack were probably part of the Arete. This was way above my pay grade. "I think I need to call the Grand Inquisitor."

Tiz swished her tail and scoffed. "What can that old battleax do? There ain't no witches on the property."

I looked at Bryant. "What about the PEB?"

He shook his head. "There's no law against shifters dabbling in magic of any kind. And like I said before, you don't want them here."

My familiar gave me a WTF look.

I gave her a slight head shake and addressed the room. "I can't just do nothing."

"For now, you have to, Haze." Ford enveloped me

in the best, warmest, most soothing bear hug. "Any action you take might be seen as giving me an unfair advantage." He tilted my head back and kissed me tenderly. "It's getting late. We're not going to figure anything out tonight. You've got Patrick and his crew watching the pack. Your officers have their orders and will call you if anything happens."

"You're right." I sighed and pressed my forehead to his chest. "Take me home."

As we left the Baylors' house that night, the stars shining coldly overhead, I couldn't shake the feeling that something bad was coming. Something big. The werewolves were just the beginning. I didn't know what Brahm Jensen was planning, but I knew one thing for certain—I wasn't going to let him tear my family or this town apart.

CHAPTER 6

THE FOLLOWING DAY, I woke up early and attempted to make breakfast. The key word here was attempted. My nerves were shot, and the result was the disaster unfolding in my kitchen.

I watched in dismay as the eggs I had just cracked into the pan sizzled and popped, the yolks bursting like tiny grenades. The toast was burning in the toaster, sending out tendrils of smoke that curled ominously toward the ceiling. And the coffee—oh, the coffee—was somehow brewing into a concoction that smelled suspiciously like something had died in it.

"Goddess in a pink tutu!" Tizzy, my ever-snarky familiar, darted around the kitchen, her tiny claws clicking against the countertop as she tried to avoid the chaos. "Hazel! Get it together, witch!" She dodged a rogue piece of toast that shot out of the toaster as if it had a mind of its own.

"I'm trying, Tiz." My magic was on the fritz, short-circuiting in response to the storm of emotions churning inside me. The Rite was set for tomorrow night, and every time I thought about what Ford was facing, my heart clenched with fear. Unfortunately, my anxiety over him was turning my appliances into my own personal Hell-version of "Maximum Overdrive."

Tizzy picked up the toast and jumped across the counter to the sink.

"Stay away from the garbage disposal!" I warned her.

The squirrel skittered backward as the blades began to churn. She clutched her chest. "Belch fire and save the matches."

"I'm sorry," I said, unable to turn it off with either magic or the switch. I shook my spatula at her. "I'm a magical disaster this morning."

"No kidding," she agreed. "Shut it down, Haze. Shut it all down."

Ford, dressed in only boxers, appeared in the doorway, drawn by the commotion. His eyes softened when he saw the mess I'd made. Without a word, he crossed the room, turned off the stove, and garbage disposal, then gently pried the spatula from my hand.

"Hazel, love, at this rate, you're going to burn the house down," he teased, though his tone held more understanding than reprimand.

"I just wanted to make you a nice breakfast," I murmured, biting my lip as I surveyed the disaster zone. "But I can't seem to get my act together this morning."

Ford set the spatula down and pulled me into his arms, his embrace warm and solid, like a fortress against the fears gnawing at me. "You're doing everything right, sweetheart," he said softly, his voice a low rumble that calmed my magic and soothed my frazzled nerves. "You're worried, and that's okay. But you need to trust that I'm going to get through this. We're going to get through this."

I buried my face in his warm, hairy chest, inhaling his familiar scent of cinnamon and spice. His scent always grounded me, no matter how chaotic things got. "I know you will," I whispered, trying to convince myself.

Ford's hand found its way to my hair, stroking it gently. "I'll kick his ass," he promised, tilting my chin up so I had to meet his gorgeous blue eyes. "But I need you to stay strong, Hazel. For both of us."

I nodded, the lump in my throat making it hard to speak. "I will," I said, forcing a smile. "I'm not worried."

But of course, I was lying. And he knew it. Ford

gave me a long, searching look before leaning down to kiss me. "I love you, Hazel. More than anything. Don't forget that."

"I love you too," I whispered.

"When do you want to come over to the courthouse?" he asked.

I tucked my chin. "The courthouse?"

"Tanya's suggestion to do a reveal spell was a good one. If Jensen is getting help from someone in town, we have to try everything we can to get to the truth."

"Oh, right." I had almost forgotten. Jensen's challenge had consumed my thoughts. "I'll come over after the briefing this morning. I need to get my officers up to speed." I laced my fingers behind his neck. "I'm sure I don't have to tell you to keep my visit under wraps. If the records disappearing was an inside job, we don't want the culprit getting a heads-up."

"I haven't been off the job that long, love." The corners of his kissable lips tugged up into a smile. "That goes without saying." His hands slid down my back to my butt, and he gave it a playful squeeze. "Go get in the shower. I'll clean up the kitchen."

"There's nothing sexier than a man offering to clean the kitchen." I grinned and squeezed his butt back. "But I say we skip the cleaning altogether, and you join me."

"Once again, this town is falling apart, and you two are hornier than dryads at the feast of Bacchus. I swear to Hades. Chaos is your choice of aphrodisiac," Tizzy complained. "Who needs oysters or rhino horns when you've got apocalyptic danger around every corner."

I almost felt guilty for a second, but then Ford laughed as he lifted me in his arms, making my lady bits sing. Guilt gone.

"Fine!" Tizzy yelled as he carried me up the stairs. "Get your sexy on. I'll clean up while you two make the hell-beast with two backs. Don't worry about me. I've got this covered. Someone has to be the grown-up around here."

She was still complaining when Ford shut the bedroom door behind us.

An hour and a half later, I was at the station and in the briefing room, feeling much, much more relaxed. However, I was the only one. I found myself facing a group of tired but attentive officers. Most of them had worked double shifts to beef up patrol and safety in town. The air was thick with unspoken questions, but I had to keep it together. My post-shower buzz waned, and I could already feel the weight of the day pressing down on me again.

"All right, everyone," I began, my voice echoing slightly in the small room. "We're in a 'watch and see' situation with Jensen and his pack of werewolves. That means no one engages unless they break the law or pose a direct threat. Clear?"

Nods and a few muttered affirmations followed, but I could see the unease on their faces. They weren't used to sitting on their hands, especially with a pack of dangerous werewolves in town. Next, I filled them in on the challenge Jensen had issued. The witches looked confused, but I could see the shifters understood the gravity of the situation.

Charity Newsome, ever the practical witch, raised her hand. "Chief, where's this rite supposed to take place?"

I hesitated. That was the million-dollar question. "Location hasn't been decided yet." I hadn't even thought about where this fight to the death would occur. "I'm going to the courthouse after the briefing, and I'll ask Ford about it."

"And if Ford loses?" someone else piped up. The question hung in the air like a bad smell.

I didn't have a good answer for that one. I swallowed the lump in my throat, forcing a smile. "We're not planning for that outcome. You all know Ford, and most of you have worked with him. You know he's as tough as they come. He's got this."

They didn't look convinced. I struggled with my fears, but I couldn't let them see that.

Suddenly, the door to the briefing room slammed open, and Bex came barreling in, breathless and wide-eyed. "Chief! We've got an incident on Harmony Street. Larry Berry's swinging a bat at some werewolves. Patrick says you need to get down there because it's getting ugly fast."

My stomach dropped. Larry Berry was a young cougar shifter with more guts than sense. If he was taking a bat to Jensen's crew, things were spiraling out of control. Translocating would be the fastest way there, but my magic was unreliable, especially now, and I didn't want to risk reappearing inside a brick wall. Luckily, Harmony was only a few minutes away by car.

"Bex, hold down the fort." I motioned for the others to follow. "Let's move."

I arrived on Harmony Street to find exactly what I'd feared. Larry was in full half-cougar mode, his clothes ripped, his skin golden-furred, and his eyes glowing with rage as he swung a metal bat at a group of sneering werewolves. Jensen, flanked by his second and beta, watched the scene with a smug grin. A dozen citizens watched from a distance, but none stepped up to try and stop the altercation. Probably for the best. I wasn't sure how the werewolves would react if more people got involved. Right now, they didn't seem to view Larry as a real threat, which was probably the only reason the boy was thus far unharmed.

I noted Pierce Roberts, a local accountant and no

fan of mine, leaning against a lamppost, his arms crossed over his chest as he watched the scene unfold as if it were an amusing game of touch football at a Sunday picnic. Roberts had been a friend of Adele's and was reluctant to believe she'd been practicing forbidden magic. On top of that, he blamed me for her death. Could he somehow be involved with the werewolves' sudden appearance in our neck of the woods? I didn't like the warlock, but he'd never given me any reason to believe he was part of Adele's cult.

"Larry, drop the bat!" I ordered, placing myself between the wolves and the young shifter.

Larry, who was beyond reason, did not drop the bat. Oish.

I waved at Officer Rhonda Petry. She was a cougar shifter like Larry. "Petry, calm him down and get him out of here."

"I'll try, Chief," Petry said. "But I'm not sure he'll listen to me any better than you."

"Just try, okay?"

The three werewolves taunting Larry laughed at our efforts, while Larry snarled and spat like an overgrown feral cat.

Meanwhile, I locked eyes with Jensen and strode over, my magic crackling beneath the surface. "Jensen!" I glared at the alpha wolf. "Get your people under control." When he didn't move, I added, "Now, before I arrest the lot of you."

"You can't arrest us," he said snidely, spreading his hands wide. "We haven't broken any laws."

I listed off the potential charges. "Disturbing the peace, intimidation, public nuisance, failure to comply with police." I glared at Jensen. "I'm sure I could think of several more that would keep you in jail for at least a week or two."

"How convenient," he said. "Using your position of power in town to try and save your mate."

"That's not what this is about," I told him, though the thought had crossed my mind. "I'm trying to de-escalate the situation. Take your pack and get out of town. No harm, no foul."

A crackling, high-pitched roar stopped all the commotion. I pivoted my gaze from Jensen to the sidewalk and saw Mary Lowe, the cat shifter alpha. "Home, Larry," she directed the young man. "And stay there until you grow some sense." Mary looked like a middle-aged housewife, but I could feel the power behind her words.

Larry complied, her command draining the fight right out of him. With a quick nod, he dropped the bat and walked away. Mary shot me a look that silently asked, "What are you going to do about this?" before she followed after the hot-headed werecougar.

I turned on Jensen, my voice low and menacing. "Get your pack out of town and back to the junkyard."

"Fine. We'll go," Jensen replied, his smile widening as he sized me up like a predator eyeing its prey. "For now. But when I kill your mate, Hazel, I'll be more than happy to pick up the pieces of your broken heart. If you're lucky, I'll even show you what it's like to have a real man in your bed."

That was the last straw. My magic surged forward, fueled by rage and instinct. Before I could think, I raised my hand and sent a lightning bolt straight into Jensen's chest. The force of the strike sent him staggering back several feet, his cocky grin replaced by a look of stunned anger.

"Leave," I growled, my voice deadly calm. "Before I do something you won't live to regret."

Jensen's eyes narrowed, but he didn't push me further. With a reluctant snarl, he circled his finger in the air, signaling his pack to retreat. "Let's go," he barked, his voice dripping with venom. As they turned to leave, he threw a glance over his shoulder, his eyes glinting with a dark promise. "I look forward to next time, Hazel."

"Next time, I'll wound more than your pride," I shot back.

I stood firm until they were out of sight, the adrenaline slowly ebbing away. Only then did I allow myself a shaky breath. I had a feeling that the next encounter wouldn't be far off, and it would be even worse than this. But for now, we'd bought ourselves a little more time, and I'd take whatever I could get.

I motioned for John Parker to join me. "I want patrols on every business street until we get rid of these jerks."

"Got it, Chief."

Later that morning, I sat in my office, reexamining all my terrible life choices. I still needed to head over to the courthouse, but I wanted to get centered first. The last thing I needed was to blow up a historical building while trying to cast a spell in public.

Bex poked her head into my office. "You okay?"

I waved her off. "All good." It was a bald-faced lie. Like a duck on water, I was calm and collected on the surface, but underneath, I was frantically paddling with both feet. "Call Patrick and get an update from his network."

As Bex left, my phone rang. The number was listed as unknown. Normally, I'd let it go to voicemail, but these weren't normal circumstances.

"Police Chief Hazel Kinsey," I answered, my tone sharp with authority.

"Hazel Kinsey?" a low, gravelly voice I didn't recognize asked.

"I just said that," I replied, my grip tightening on the phone. "Who's calling?"

"Let's just say I'm someone who knows what's coming your way," the voice said. "And if you care about your man, you'll listen carefully."

My heart skipped a beat. "Who are you?"

"Someone who knows Brahm Jensen," the caller said, his tone sharp with bitterness. "And I know what he's planning, and it's not just about claiming territory. It's about power—power he's been gathering from a source you can't imagine."

"What do you mean?" I asked, my mind racing. "What kind of power?"

"Brahm has no plans to lose to your mate tomorrow night," the caller continued. "Taking over your town is just the beginning."

"How do I know you're telling the truth?"

"I'm in his pack," the stranger said.

"Then why are you telling me this?"

"Because some of us don't like where Jensen is taking us," he growled, frustration clear in his voice. "This was a mistake."

"Wait," I insisted. "If you're serious—"

"I am."

Harvest in a hailstorm, I hadn't expected an informant from Jensen's ranks to fall into my lap. "Then tell me what you know."

"I can't do it over the phone," the caller replied. "If you want to save your mate and your town, you'll have to meet me somewhere private. Come alone. If anyone shows up with you, I'll leave, and you won't get any more information from me."

"You'll bring proof that Jensen is up to no good?" I asked, hope sparking in my chest. If I could get real evidence, I might be able to stop the challenge before it even began.

"Yes," the man said. "I have proof that he'll do anything to win."

"You mean he's going to cheat during the Rite of Arphlition," I clarified.

A soft exhale, then he spelled it out. "Yes, he plans to use forbidden magic to win."

This seemed too good to be true, but I wanted to believe that one of Jensen's men would turn on him. If it could save Ford, I had to try. "Where do you want to meet?"

"I'll text when I can slip away unnoticed. It will be later tonight. Keep your phone handy."

The line went dead before I could ask anything more. I sat there, the phone still pressed to my ear, my thoughts swirling like a hurricane. Jensen had a turncoat in his group. That was the only advantage I had right now. The mention of forbidden magic aligned with what Tizzy had sensed at the junkyard garage. The werewolves were up to something nefarious, and one thing was clear—I needed answers, and I needed them before the supermoon tomorrow night.

CHAPTER 7

AT A LITTLE PAST ELEVEN, I crossed the street to the courthouse. Its solid, fortress-like structure dominated the view. The building's dark, rough-hewn stone walls rose imposingly, making me feel suddenly small. The earlier fiasco with Jensen was still fresh in my mind—I couldn't believe I'd actually zapped him. Luckily, my magic hadn't done any severe or lasting damage to the alpha jerkwad because, technically, zapping someone just for running their mouth is a big no-no in the witch world. With everything else going on, the last thing I wanted was a visit from the Grand Inquisitor herself, aka Clementine Battles, aka my grandmother, for being a naughty witch.

Inside the front door, on the left, was the assessor's office. Down the narrow corridor and on the right was the door for the county clerk. I hoped Tyris

Chestnut hadn't left for his lunch break yet because I needed him to point me in the direction of where the records would've been before they went missing. The old hardwood floors creaked under my weight. Ford rounded the corner at the end of the hall, his brow dipped in consternation.

"You confronted Jensen." It wasn't a question.

"In my defense, he confronted me. I was just doing my job."

"You used your magic on him."

"Because he begged me to do it," I countered.

Ford's brows went up. "He begged you?" This time it was a question.

I didn't want to tell Ford what the werewolf had said about showing me what a real man is like in bed. Jensen hadn't been flirting. He'd said it as a threat to intimidate me. On some level, it had worked. "He said some really nasty crap, and in my book, when you talk smack, you're asking for a smack." I gave my husband a quick hug. "Besides, he's fine. No harm, no foul."

Ford shook his head. "I can't have it appear that your magic gives me an advantage. It could put the outcome in dispute when I win."

I smiled. I liked that he said "when" and not "if." He believed in his ability to beat Jensen, and I believed in him. My fear wasn't that Ford wasn't strong enough or skilled enough to beat Jensen in a fair fight. It was the fact that since I'd moved back to Paradise Falls, I was always a little afraid. Before, when I was with the FBI, I was a door kicker. The first one into a room. As much as I wanted to catch bad guys, and that was a biggie, I also got a rush from the danger. After losing my parents, regardless of the reasons, I'd put up walls to keep myself from getting hurt like that again. The walls had made me feel invincible—someone who had nothing to lose. Finding Ford again and finding out he was my mate changed my world into something unbelievably beautiful and precious. Our life together was more wonderful than I ever imagined, and I was always scared that something would happen to take it all away from me.

I met my husband's bright-eyed gaze. "I'm sorry, Ford."

His expression turned curious. "For what, love?"

My voice cracked with emotion. "For being a control freak with trust and abandonment issues."

He cracked a smile. "It's part of your charm."

I rolled my eyes and shoved down the ever-present urge to bear-nap him to another country until the bad stuff passed. Contrary to pie-in-the-sky thinking, bad stuff didn't go away on its own accord. It took action. So, action I would take. "Come on," I told him. "I've got a spell to cast."

Ford opened the door to the clerk's office, and we

stepped inside. The air was thick with the scent of old, musty paper and ink. Tall metal filing cabinets lined the back walls, their labels faded and hard to read. A long, polished wooden counter stretched across the front of the room, worn smooth from years of use. Behind the counter sat Tyris Chestnut, the lanky warlock clerk. He'd been the county clerk for as long as I could remember. I couldn't forget his kindness when, at eighteen, I'd had to file my mother's death certificate. It had been a necessary step before selling off our family's assets after Dad's incarceration. I'd sold everything—our home, our vehicles—and used the money to escape Paradise Falls.

Tyris glanced up from a stack of folders and pushed his round glasses up the bridge of his nose. As a warlock, he hadn't needed glasses. Poor vision wasn't something our kind had to worry about. His unruly brown hair and dark brown eyes completed the look of a small-town clerk. There was something comforting in his appearance. It's probably why he kept getting elected to the position.

"Hello, Mayor." He nodded to Ford then smiled genially at me. "Chief," he greeted. "What can I do for you both today?"

"Hazel is going to cast a spell to see if she can figure out what happened to the missing files."

Tyris grimaced. "In all my years, I've never lost

any files." He shook his head. "At least none that I've known about. After this, though, I've decided to go through every record in my office to see if anything else is gone." He gestured to the stack of folders he'd been tending to. "It'll take me a few years to get through all of them, but days are slow, and I've got nothing but time."

The Goddess had granted him the patience of a saint. The idea of trudging through a couple hundred years of files made me want to crawl out of my skin. It definitely took all kinds to make the world work. "I'm pretty good with reveal spells," I told him. "I might be able to expose a clue that would give us an idea of what happened to the files."

"Not the who?" he queried.

"My witch specialty doesn't work like that, unfortunately." All witches had one or two things they were gifted at when it came to their abilities. Mine happened to work well with my chosen profession and was really the only spellcasting I was confident about.

"Sure," Tyris said. "What do you need from me?"

I gestured to the shelves. "Just point me in the direction where the files should've been. I can take it from there."

"Should I leave?" he asked.

I shook my head. "You can stay."

He walked to one of the tall filing cabinets in the

center of the back wall. "Here's where the property deeds are kept in these two cabinets. They are filed by address, not names, and Driver's property is in the county section with the rural route addresses." He gestured to three of the filing drawers. "Since Paradise Falls is the only town in the county, there isn't as many rural addresses as town ones." He scrubbed a hand over his hair, mussing it even more. Maybe his unruly appearance was less calculated than I'd thought. He opened the middle drawer. "The property is 501 SE 82, so it should've been in this area between the four hundreds and the end of the seven hundreds."

"You remember the address?"

"I looked it up yesterday, but even if I hadn't, I remember every piece of paperwork I file. It's my magical gift. I have perfect recall."

Huh. I hadn't known that about Tyris. What I did know was that the 501 in Driver's address indicated that it was five miles from our post office it was and that eighty-two was the street address. "Could you have misfiled it in the section where you keep the addresses under a hundred?"

He gave me a don't-be-a-silly-witch look. "I would never misfile my records." He tapped his temple. "Like I said, perfect recall."

All righty then. "Well, then, if you don't mind,

you and Ford should go to the other side of the counter." I shrugged. "You know, just in case."

Tyris' eyes widened with alarm. "I don't know. What's just in case?"

Ford put his hand on the thin man's shoulders and gave him a slight head shake. "It'll be fine. Hazel knows what she's doing."

"Absolutely," I reassured the keeper of records. "There's no problem." Aside from a few unpredictabilities, like turning my kitchen into a horror movie and accidentally electrocuting a werewolf. "This will be easy peasy."

He didn't look assured.

Ford patted his shoulder and ushered him around the counter to the other side. "Let's give Hazel room to work, okay?"

I stared at the file drawers and sent a silent Hail Mary prayer to the Goddess not to blow anything up. After, I cleared the clutter from my brain and concentrated on the work at hand. I was an investigator. This was my calling. I had this.

My second sight allowed me to see things at a crime scene that no one else could. If something was important, it would glow for me. Luckily, I was the only one who could see the glow, so I'd used it many times on my FBI cases in the mundane human world.

"Goddess, bring me second sight.

Turn the darkness into light.
What once was filed is now missing.
Reveal a path, make the unseen seen.
Done and done, Goddess grant to me,
Second sight, so mote it be."

I did a little victory dance when nothing went kablooey. The file drawer where Driver's land deed had been filed glowed as I had expected. What I hadn't expected was the six other file drawers that had also lit up.

"What's going on?" I heard Tyris ask. "Nothing happened."

Ford said, "Oh, yes it did."

I pointed to the glowing drawers. "What files are in these?"

"Those four on the immediate left are residential housing, and the other two are filings for birth certificates," he answered.

"If you're looking to see what else is missing, start with these." I waggled my finger at the wall. "I'm pretty sure someone has either removed or added files to these drawers."

"Why would they do that?" he asked.

I shrugged. "For the same reason, they removed Clayton Driver's deed. To hide something they don't want us to find out."

I scanned the rest of the office to make sure I wasn't missing anything. A leatherbound book at the end of the long counter had a faint pulsing glow. "What's that?" I asked Tyris as I made my way there.

"It's a ledger. When someone wants access to the public records, they must sign them in and out."

I frowned. "That would've been good information to have earlier." I opened the large-ish tome. "Does it list what records they access?"

Tyris nodded. "Yes, but there's no telling when they would have."

"What about your perfect recall?" I asked.

"Unfortunately, it's only for the files, not the people. I have a terrible memory for names and faces."

"Can you think of anyone who would've wanted to look at Clayton Driver's land deed?"

He shook his head. "No, but I really don't think anyone could have removed files while I was here. That I would've noticed."

A thought occurred to me. "What about Adele Abbot?"

Tyris narrowed his gaze, his eyes crinkling at the corners. "What about her?"

Ford picked up on where I was going. "Has anyone accessed her records since her death?" he asked.

"Only one person that I know of," the clerk told us.

"Who?" I couldn't keep the eagerness out of my tone. "Who wanted her records?"

"Golda Gedes," he replied.

"Golda?" She was on the council and one of the oldest witches in town. Could she have been in on the Arete stuff with Adele? I didn't want to believe it, but at this point I couldn't afford not to track down every lead. "Thanks for your help, Tyris." I gestured to the file drawers I'd pointed out. "Could you look through those first and tell me what, if anything, is missing?"

He nodded. "I will do that, Chief."

"Thanks for your help," I told the disheveled warlock. "I appreciate it."

"Just doing my civic duty." He gave me a cute little salute.

As Ford and I left the clerk's office, he said, "I guess we're going to see Golda."

"Smart bear." I linked my arm in his. "You guessed right."

CHAPTER 8

GOLDA GEDES LIVED in the same sprawling neighborhood as us. We bought our ornate yet comfortable Victorian house after the previous owner, Agatha Milan, had died under mysterious circumstances. Golda's house, like ours, was Victorian in style. The door, a dark, rich mahogany, looked more expensive than my last three vacations combined. I rang the doorbell, and deep, low chimes played a lyrical Irish air.

A few seconds later, Golda opened the door.

"Hazel, Ford," she greeted us with a warm smile. "This is an unexpected surprise."

Golda's brown hair, soft and voluminous, was pulled into a loose bun on top of her head. She had kind eyes and smooth skin. She was curvier than most witches and in all the right places. Even at over a hundred years old, she was beautiful.

"Hi, Ms. Gedes," I said, more formally than I'd planned. "We just have a few questions we'd like to ask you."

"Well, don't stand there letting the pixies in," she said. "Come in, come in." She led us through the foyer to a sitting room. Much like the last time I visited, her sitting room was filled with stacks of books, maps, and many impressive relics. She had revealed the witch ancestry of my friend Lily Mason, a cougar shifter. Lily had developed a witch power, and Golda, as the town's historian, knew exactly which witch Lily had inherited her lie-detector magic from. "Can I get you a cup of tea or something?"

"I'm good," Ford said.

"Same," I told her. "But thank you."

"You're welcome, dear. Will you at least have a seat?" She didn't wait for us to accept her offer before sitting in a high-backed, velvet-cushioned chair across from Ford and me. Golda's brown eyes, usually filled with warmth, now held a guarded look as she waited for us to speak. "What can I do for you both?"

I cleared my throat, choosing my words carefully. "Golda, you know what's going on with the were-wolves in town and how they might have been part of a secret society, the same as Adele Abbot."

"Yes," she said. "I was at the meeting last night,

same as you. What is this about? Do you need information about the town's history regarding Adele?"

"That's not the information I'm looking for." I gave her an assessing stare, wanting to gauge her reaction to my next question. "Why did you request access to Adele's files at the courthouse?"

The question hung in the air, and I watched Golda's expression flicker—just for a moment—before she smiled gently. "I've always been a chronicler for Paradise Falls. I keep records of all the families, new and old. When Adele died, I needed her files to finish her family page. She was an only child, never married, and had no children. Her death marked the end of the Abbot line. I needed the physical records to accurately record the final chapter of the Abbot family history."

Her explanation made a lot of sense, but I couldn't shake the feeling that she was withholding something.

Ford's voice was calm but probing. "What about Clayton Driver?"

Golda leaned back in her chair, her gaze steady on Ford. "What about that fool?"

I nodded slowly, trying to piece together the puzzle. "Did you look at his records? Specifically, the land deed?"

"No," she denied. "I only keep track of the witch

families." She scooted forward in her chair. "What is this really about?"

Golda was a no-nonsense woman, so I decided to be direct. "I told the coalition yesterday afternoon that Clayton Driver's land deed went missing from the county clerk's office. I think it could be evidence that Brahm Jensen and his pack are illegally occupying the Junkyard Dog and the surrounding land using a forged document. Since Clayton died at the same time as Adele, I wondered if there would be a reason for you to have taken a look?"

The historian's brow furrowed, her fingers tapping lightly on the armrest. "Am I some kind of suspect?"

"No," I admitted. "Not at this time. But I have to follow every lead."

Ford leaned forward, his tone impatient. "Did you have anything to do with the missing deed, Ms. Gedes?"

"Why would I?" Her placid expression didn't waver. Golda was one cool customer.

"Adele and you were friends, right?" he pressed. "Maybe more. If the deed was important to the Arete, maybe you thought it was better kept out of reach—kept secret to be used at a later date when the Arete could be revived."

Golda's eyes widened slightly, and for the first

time, her composure cracked. "No, I would never... Hazel, Ford, I understand your concerns, but I had nothing to do with the Arete or that deed disappearing. My only interest has been in protecting our town from the remnants of the Arete's influence."

"So you admit that the records you looked at had something to do with the Arete," I said.

"Yes, fine," she acknowledged. "I didn't want anyone stumbling across Adele's legacy accidentally. I'd heard rumors that she kept a secret place where she practiced dark arts. I didn't want it discovered. Ever. This town has suffered enough."

I exchanged a glance with Ford, both of us assessing her words. There was something in her voice—an earnestness that was hard to fake—but we'd been burned before by those who seemed trustworthy.

"Golda," I said, my voice softer, "we need to know everything if we're going to prevent whatever's happening. If you have any other information, anything at all, it could be vital."

She looked at me for a long moment, then sighed, her shoulders sagging slightly. "There's one more thing. When I reviewed Adele's records, I found a reference to a specific ritual site." She wrung her hands. "I believe it's where the Arete conducted some of their most powerful ceremonies. The location was never mentioned explicitly, but I believe it's connected to Clayton Driver's land."

Ford stiffened beside me. "Do you know where this site is?"

Golda shook her head. "I don't, but if someone is trying to find it, that could explain why they'd want to erase any trace of the real deed. If the land was used for those rituals, it could hold significant power —a power that could be exploited."

A cold chill ran down my spine. "If that's true, then whoever has the deed might be planning to use that power."

"I should've said something at the meeting yesterday, but I wasn't sure if the information would help or make things worse. After a hundred years of keeping history, I've hidden many family secrets from being exposed." The way she looked at me after saying "family secrets" made me think she was talking about my family.

I didn't have the emotional bandwidth to deal with ancient family drama. Getting Jensen the hell out of town was the only goal. "This secret about Driver's property is one that shouldn't have been kept," I stated flatly. "You should've told us."

"I want to help." Golda looked genuinely troubled, her earlier composure replaced by deep concern. "If there's anything I can do, I will. But please, be careful. The Arete's magic is twisted and cursed. If this werewolf pack are practitioners, then everyone in town is in danger."

I nodded. "Thank you, Golda. We'll be in touch if we need anything else."

As we left her sitting room, I couldn't shake the feeling that she was still holding something back—whether out of fear or guilt, I wasn't sure. But one thing was certain: the missing land deed was more than just a piece of paper. It was the key to unlocking a bleak chapter of our town's past. A chapter I never wanted to revisit.

As we returned to the car, I couldn't shake the nagging thought that Golda might be more involved than she let on. I glanced at Ford, who was already wearing that expression I'd come to recognize—he was thinking the same thing.

"Ford, what if Golda was part of the Arete? If not now, then in the past?" I asked, my voice low as we reached the car. "Or at least had ties to them?"

He paused with his hand on the door handle. "It crossed my mind too. She knew way more about Adele and the Arete than she let on initially. And if she's had access to those records, who's to say she didn't do more than just protect them?"

I leaned against the car, running a hand through my hair. "Exactly. She was quick to downplay her involvement, but what if she's been covering her tracks? Or worse, what if she's the reason the were-wolves are here? How do you open a town to chaos? Dethrone the leaders. That's us."

Ford nodded, his expression grim. "We need to figure out her role in all of this." He opened the door for me, and I slid into the passenger seat. He rounded the sedan and got in on the other side.

"Maybe Golda is what she says she is, or maybe she's an Arete mastermind," I said as he started the engine. "Either way, we can't take her word at face value."

"Agreed." Ford glanced at the house, then back at me.

"If she's right about Adele's secret ritual site, then Clayton's land is crucial to whatever plan this cult has in the works," I mused. "And if Golda knew that…" I trailed off, the implications settling heavily.

"Then she'd have every reason to make sure that deed disappeared." Ford backed out of the driveway. "We'll need to look into Golda's past, her connections, everything."

"And we need to do it quietly," I added. "If she's involved, we can't let her know we're onto her. She might have more tricks up her sleeve."

Ford's jaw tightened, a sure sign he was ready for action. "I'll start with the town's archives, see what I can find on her and her connections.

And I'll touch base with Tyris and see if he's found anything missing from those other drawers."

"Good plan." I nodded, trying to shake off the unease that clung to me. "But Ford... be careful. We might be dealing with more than just hidden records."

He gave me a reassuring smile, though I could see the worry in his eyes. "You too, Hazel."

There was a pall of silence for a minute or two as we headed back into town, broken when Ford muttered, "Jensen stopped by the courthouse earlier today."

The hair on the back of my neck stood up. "Before the street incident with Larry Berry?"

"About half an hour before," he said.

"And you're just telling me now?"

"Yeah, sorry. He wanted to firm up the spot where the rite will take place."

My chest squeezed. "And did the spot get firmed?"

"Paradise Falls Park. The open field near the lake."

"No," I groaned. "That's where we got married." Granted, not before spilling some blood in a deadly showdown with a homicidal wedding crasher. "Can't you pick somewhere else?"

"It is a place of power for shifters." His eyes softened. "And for me, I have a strong bond to the place because it's where we exchanged vows."

"Home field advantage, huh?"

He gave me a reassuring smile. "Exactly."

"Fine." I sighed. I was good with anything that gave Ford the edge he needed to win. I set my hand on his thigh and squeezed. "Go team."

CHAPTER 9

I SPENT the rest of the afternoon putting out fires at work. Peeling my skin off would be counterproductive, so I just did my damned job. My officers confirmed that Jensen and his pack had left town, but we were getting a flood of "sighting" calls from worried citizens. On top of that, complaints were piling up. Word of the challenge had spread to the citizens of Paradise Falls, and they were scared, especially in the shifter community. The witches, who didn't have to follow the furry-kin's rules, would continue doing their own thing, but the shifters under Bryant would have to either fall in line under Jensen's rule or find a new place to live.

By the time I got home, I felt brain-drained and insane. Ford was in the kitchen, his back to me as he worked with a skillet on the stove. The smell of bacon filled the air, a comforting reminder of normalcy. He greeted me with a weary smile.

"Tough afternoon?" he asked, removing the bacon from the frying pan and setting it on some paper towels to drain.

"Non-stop calls from concerned citizens." I forced a smile. "You?"

"Same. Word has spread around town." His blue eyes sparkled with amusement. "Good thing it's not an election year."

"Barnstable Bear's not wrong," Tizzy said, popping up on the center island. She grabbed an almond from the bowl of mixed nuts Ford had set out. "Right now, he'd struggle to get elected head garbage collector." She cracked the shell. "Of course, if he manages to take out the werewolf trash…"

"Uh, hold up," I said. "Who's Barnstable Bear?" I usually got all of Tizzy's endearments for my honey-pot, but this one went over my head.

"He's from a comic strip." She gave me a 'duh' look. "Came out in the fifties. Barnstable was a grizzly bear that was short-tempered, not too bright…" The squirrel shook her head. "Never mind. If I have to explain it, it loses its punch."

I caught Ford trying not to laugh out of the corner of my eye as he sliced up a large beefsteak tomato. Yum. We were having BLTs for dinner. "Did you need something?" I asked her.

"Can't a squirrel just stop in to say hello?"

I was beginning to wonder if something else was going on with Tizzy. She'd been showing up out of the blue a lot, and without "the love of her life," Lupita, the stupid cat. "Is everything okay, Tiz?" I asked her. "I mean, between you and Loopy-doopy?"

"All good." She waved off my concern. "Couldn't be better."

I remained unconvinced, but I wouldn't force her if she didn't want to talk about it. "Want to stay for dinner?"

"I'm not here for a pity meal," she quipped. "I just wanted to tell you about something I saw at the restaurant today."

"Oh, what's that?"

"Pierce Roberts and Sally Teeter were at the restaurant this afternoon, and I overheard them talking about Robert Townsend."

Robert Townsend used to be the head of the small shifter faction, and he'd been Adele Abbots' right hand in her dark magic cult. He'd always owned a real estate company, Wonderland Realty. Sally had been his secretary-slash-associate at the time. Since his demise, Sally had taken over running the business. She'd even sold Ford our house after Agatha's estate had come out of probate.

"What about Townsend?" Ford asked, getting the bread from the cupboard.

"Pierce said he'd heard that Townsend had acquired some property southeast of town near the Lister County line, and he wanted to know if Sally would sell it to him."

This seemed to connect a little too closely with what Golda had said about Adele having property near the junkyard. "What did Sally say?"

"She told him she'd look into it, but she didn't seem happy about it." Tizzy grabbed a walnut from the bowl. "I got the impression she didn't like Pierce much."

"What's to like?" I quipped. "The man has a stick up his butt the size of a telephone pole."

"True that," Tizzy agreed. "Soon after, Sally put ten bucks on the table for her meal and left. She'd only eaten half her sandwich and didn't bother to take the other half to go."

"Maybe it was the food," I teased.

Tizzy clutched her chest, and with the flair of a Shakespearean-trained thespian, she cried, "Oh, Hazel. You wound me."

"Whatever." I rolled my eyes. "So, did they arrive together?"

"I don't think so." She chewed on the nut for a moment, then added, "Sally looked annoyed when he sat at her table."

"Good to know." Had Pierce been involved with Adele's dark dealings? I disliked the man, but I had never really suspected him. "As far as I'm concerned, he's on the suspect list now." I turned to Ford. "Did Tyris find anything missing?"

He grabbed the mayo from the fridge and started making our sandwiches. "Tyris said that Adele's property records were missing along with Robert Townsend's, and, weirdly, a sealed adoption form."

"For who?"

"He didn't know. The adoption forms are sealed before he gets them. He files them in their section with the birth certificates. They're numbered so that if an adoptee wants to find their birth parent, they can, as long as the birth parent has given permission. In this case, the record was to be permanently sealed."

"Wild," I said, taking the sandwich he'd made for me. "If it's sealed, who would take it?"

"The kid? The birth parent?" Tizzy said. "They would have the most reason."

I shrugged. "Yeah, but how would they know which one to take?" I took a bite, savoring the mix of sun-ripened tomato, smoky bacon, crisp lettuce, and salty mayo. "It doesn't make sense."

"Sense or not, it's what we got," Ford said.

The clues were vague, and the odds of us figuring out what Jensen was up to and getting the proof needed to stop him were insurmountable. I had my phone in my pocket, set to vibrate, just in case the anonymous informant texted me. I wanted to tell Ford. I hated keeping secrets from him. But Deep Throat had told me he would only meet me alone, and I knew that if I told Ford, there was no way I could keep him away from it. I had to take the chance if there was even the slightest possibility that Jensen had a turncoat in his ranks. Was it dangerous to go alone? Yes. But I knew how to take care of myself. Besides, I could apparate out of the situation if things got hinky.

At least that's how I was rationalizing my lie-by-omission. At this point, I wondered if the guy had been blowing smoke up my butt. He hadn't texted, and I was beginning to suspect the call had been a prank.

Ford sat down on the stool beside mine. He nudged me with his shoulder. "Penny for your thoughts."

"I'm frustrated, is all." I leaned against him. "It seems the more we find out, the less we know." I stared out the window at the darkening sky. "And we're running out of time." Tomorrow was D-day.

Tizzy took a couple more nuts and said, "Thanks for dinner, Boo Boo."

Ford grinned. "Anytime, Scrat." Scrat was the saber-tooth squirrel from the *Ice Age* movies, and I could tell my husband was quite pleased with his comeback.

I shook my head. "Thanks for the info, Tiz. You're the best."

"You got it." Her tail flicked back and forth at the compliment. "Welp, I better get home. Don't want to keep the missus waiting." On that note, she popped out again.

"I'm worried about her," I told him.

"Why?"

"I get the feeling something is going wrong in her personal life. I mean, I haven't seen Lupita in over a week. She and Tiz are usually joined at the hip, but Tiz keeps showing up without her."

He frowned. "Huh. You should ask your dad about it. Lupita's his familiar. Maybe he can shed some light on the situation. Then you'll know how best to help Tizzy."

I pivoted on the stool so that our knees touched. "You are the sweetest man. All that squirrel does is make fun of you, but here you are trying to help me help her."

"She loves you. You love her. When she's happy, you're happy. Of course, I want to help." Ford's eyes softened as he looked at me. He cupped my chin. "I'd do anything to make you happy, Hazel. You're my mate. My life."

Goddess, I loved the man more than words could ever express. I slid my hand over the bulge in his pants. "If you're in a helping mood, you can help me out of my clothes."

"Woman," Ford growled.

"Man." I laughed. "Race you upstairs. Loser gets sex."

"And the winner?"

"Same."

He grinned. "Win-win."

Before he could get up, I jumped to my feet and sprinted toward the stairs. Ford was hot on my heels, but I blocked his path so he couldn't get around me. We were laughing like carefree lovers when we reached our bedroom. I won our race by a fraction of a second by leaping the last few feet to land on the bed before he could get through the door.

"I win," I said.

He stripped his shirt over his head, his firm muscles flexing and rippling under his hairy chest. His eyes were dark with the promise of dirty, filthy, wonderful things.

"We'll call it a tie."

My husband was a total smoke show. Holy macaroni, he still took my breath away. "Deal," I rasped, my throat suddenly dry.

He crawled over me, his mouth melding to mine. As the kiss deepened, the world outside our bedroom ceased to exist. Ford's touch was passionate, commanding, and possessive. We lost ourselves in each other, finding solace in our connection. We made love as if our lives depended on it, as if it were the last time.

Goddess, I prayed, *don't let it be the last time.*

As the night wore on, and after several spectacular orgasms, we both drifted into a peaceful sleep, wrapped in each other's arms.

A little after two in the morning, my phone vibrated off the nightstand, jolting me awake. Groggy and disoriented, I reached for it and saw I had a text message from "Unknown."

My heart skipped a beat as I sat up.

"Who is it?" Ford mumbled, stirring beside me.

"Work," I told him. I kissed his cheek. "Go back to sleep." When he rolled over, I slipped out of bed and headed to the bathroom to read the message.

Paradise Falls Park, the text read. *Now. Hurry. Can't stay long. Remember, come alone or you get nothing.*

The park? That was the site for the challenge tomorrow night. Was that the reason for the place? The man had said he had proof Jensen would cheat. Was the evidence there? Had he done something to the area, used the druidic magic to his advantage? I had to find out. There was no other choice.

I glanced over at my hunkilicious man's sleeping

figure on the bed as I gathered some clean clothes and sneakers. Then, I went back into the bathroom and closed the door between us. I quickly got dressed, and with a heavy heart, I murmured a few magic words that I hoped would translocate me to the lake.

I reappeared, ankle-deep, in lake water. Ugh.

I stepped onto dry land and searched the area. I saw the pavilion where Ford and I had exchanged our vows and something glowing like a beacon in the distance near the hillside. Cautiously, I made my way over, keeping to the shadows when possible. Where was this guy? Why hadn't he shown himself? I reached into my pocket for my phone to text the informant and let him know I'd arrived, but it was gone.

Son-of-a-brownie biter. I'd screwed up the translocation spell again, and this time my phone was the victim. Fudge knuckles!

I made my way toward the beacon, an staggered back, my body going numb with shock when I saw the horror show on display.

The moon, large and bright, cast light over a large pentagram chalked onto the ground. Its lines appeared to glow. At the center of the pentagram lay a body staked down with a large, scorched hole in his chest. The scent of charred flesh sickened me. On top of that, the person's face had been covered with a dark cloth.

Oh, Goddess. Had my informant been discovered? Was this retribution?

I made my way over, careful not to disturb the chalk lines or any other evidence. I had to see who was under the cloth.

Slowly, I lifted the fabric from the dead man's face.

Brahm Jensen? Crap on toast. I had not seen this coming. The shock was overwhelming, and before I could process what I was seeing, I heard the distant wail of sirens. Who had called the police? Was it the informant? The fact that I'd been texted to come now to discover the body, and the cops had been called smelled of a setup. It didn't help that Jensen had a Hazel's sized hole zapped through his chest.

I winced.

Did I already zap the man once in the chest today?

Yes.

Did I imply I'd kill him the next time he came at me?

Yes.

Now that I was standing over the body, did I look guilty as hell?

Absolutely, yes.

Fuuuudddge. I could run, but I wouldn't. My officers knew and trusted me. Besides, running would make me look guiltier than I already looked.

Instead, I sat tight as the sirens grew louder and waited for my officers to arrive.

CHAPTER 10

JOHN PARKER and Mitzy Thomas were the first to arrive at the scene. The moment they stepped into the clearing, their faces contorted with the same horror that churned in my gut. Parker's eyes, wide with disbelief, locked onto mine.

"What did you do, Chief?" he demanded, his voice thick with accusation.

Mitzy shot him a sharp look, her hand coming down in a quick, warning gesture. "We don't know she did this," she reminded him firmly.

"This wasn't me," I snapped, trying to keep my voice steady as I gestured to the gruesome scene before us. "I showed up to find Jensen like this."

Parker's skepticism didn't fade. He crossed his arms over his chest, brow furrowed. "Not to sound like I don't trust you, Chief, but I seem to recall a similar hole in your wedding planner's chest."

A memory I'd rather forget flashed through my mind—my wedding planner, her chest a smoking ruin after she'd tried to shoot me with a gun. I'd acted in self-defense, but the outcome was the same. But this—Jensen's lifeless body, staked to the ground on a pentagram—this wasn't my doing.

"Well, this time it wasn't me." I did my best to keep my voice level. I wasn't sure it was working. "How did you all get here so fast? I arrived just a few minutes ago. Did you get a call to come to the park?" I asked, needing to understand how they'd ended up here so quickly.

Mitzy hesitated, glancing at Parker before meeting my gaze. "Yes, Chief," she replied, her tone reluctant. "The caller said they witnessed you murdering Jensen. They described it as some kind of forbidden ritual."

My heart pounded like a jackhammer in my chest. I scanned the scene again. Jensen's body was indeed positioned in a way that looked disturbingly ritualistic, the stakes pinning him down in a precise pattern. I could definitly see how it would look damning.

"Are you sure the caller identified me as the culprit?" I asked, my voice edged with a rising panic.

"Yes," Mitzy confirmed, her expression troubled. "Dispatch called John since he's had the most time on the job."

I spread my hands. "Look, if I had done this, I

certainly wouldn't have stuck around to see how it played out."

"I called Dr. Gellar," Parker added. "There's a team on the way to gather forensics."

"Good," I managed to say, swallowing the bile rising in my throat. I needed to take control of this scene, gather evidence, and prove that I wasn't the one who had done this. "Mitzy, start cordoning off the area. John take photos. Document everything. We need to secure—"

"I'm afraid you can't coordinate the crime scene, Chief," Parker interrupted, his voice tense.

I narrowed my gaze at him, my patience fraying. "On whose order?"

"Mine," came a cold, authoritative voice from behind me.

I spun around to see Clementine Battles, the Grand Inquisitor. Her silver hair was pulled into a severe bun, and her black pantsuit radiated authority. When it came to witches, she was the rule of law —judge, jury, and executioner, if need be.

"You can't be here, Hazel," she said, her tone as unyielding as iron. "Go home."

My eyes flicked back to Parker, my jaw tightening. "You called my grandmother?"

"I had to, Chief," he admitted, his tone almost apologetic.

Clementine stepped forward, her gaze sharp. "Be

glad he did, granddaughter. You can't be seen as trying to cover up a crime committed against an alpha werewolf who has declared the *Rite of Arphlitian* against your mate. Not unless you want a Beastwarden showing up and taking him away."

"Why would they take Ford away if I'm the guilty one?" I demanded, my voice rising with frustration.

"Because you're his mate," Clementine replied, her voice like a knife. "Your interference will look as if you've interceded on his behalf. The werewolves will seize his territory, and Paradise Falls will be lost."

My throat tightened, strangling me with my own arrogance. If I hadn't been so desperate to find evidence against Jensen, I never would've come to the park alone. There would have been witnesses to my innocence to counter the fake 9-1-1 call. Even so, I knew my grandmother was right. If it looked like I was meddling in this investigation, it would be all the excuse the werewolves needed to bring in a Beastwarden. They would come for Ford. I hated that my choice to lie to him, even if I had been trying to protect him, could cost him everything. Cost me everything too.

"What a bunch of crap," I muttered, fury and helplessness warring within me. But deep down, I knew she was right. I couldn't afford to make a single misstep, not with so much at stake. Jensen's death, the implications for Ford, and the potential loss of Paradise Falls, it all weighed heavily on me.

Other officers had started to arrive, along with a few civilian vehicles that had followed the lights and sirens. By sunrise, the news of Brahm Jensen's demise would be the talk of the town. I could see the headline now, *Ritualized Revenge: Rogue Chief Murders Werewolf Alpha*. The story practically wrote itself.

"What can I do?" I asked her. I wanted to tell her about the text message, but without my phone, I had no proof I was telling the truth. Even so, I couldn't do nothing. "I can't sit on my thumbs while my name is raked over the coals. How can anyone think that I did this?"

Clementine's gaze softened slightly, a rare glimmer of sympathy in her otherwise stern demeanor. "The facts will be revealed. If you're innocent, I will prove it."

"If?" My head felt like it would explode. "And as to the facts being revealed, it certainly didn't play out that way when you put my dad in jail for a murder he didn't commit."

Her expression steeled again. "Because Kent wasn't honest with me," she quipped. "I have to stay impartial to do my job effectively."

"Grandmother of the year," I muttered.

"Go home, Hazel. Let me handle this investigation. If you want to protect Ford and this town, you must step back."

I knew my words had hurt her, and I was sorry for that, but she was not instilling me with a whole lot of confidence at the moment. "You're not even giving me a chance to explain—"

She cut me off. "Later. I understand your frustration. I'll come by when I'm finished here and get your statement."

I clenched my fists, every instinct screaming at me to stay, to fight, to clear my name. But Clementine Battles was the law, and defying her would only make things worse.

As the Grand Inquisitor left me standing there, reeling from her cold dismissal, I saw my father striding toward me with Tanya Gellar, the medical examiner, at his side. The familiar sight of him offered a sliver of comfort. He looked worried, though, making the lines on his face deepen. The small comfort quickly faded.

"Hazel," he greeted me, his voice low and filled with concern. "Tanya woke me up when she got the call. Are you okay? What happened?"

"Dad, this wasn't me," I said, feeling desperate. I needed him to believe me, even if no one else did.

He nodded, placing a reassuring hand on my shoulder. "I believe you, Hazel. You can be impulsive, but I know you would never do..." he pointed at the scene, "that." He shook his head. "It might not be enough to stop the Witch-Shifter Coalition from convening a public hearing to review your competency as chief while this investigation plays out."

"How many people know about this already?" A wave of dread washed over me. A public hearing could ruin everything. Even if I was innocent, the scrutiny alone could destroy my career, my life, and everything I'd worked so hard to protect. Hell, right now, it wasn't looking like I'd even have a life to protect.

"Golda Gedes called me to see if it was true, that you'd killed the werewolf alpha. I told her it was balderdash. Then I got a call from Mary Lowe, Steve Crandell, and..." he paused for a moment. "Bryant."

Oh, Goddess. My father-in-law knew about the situation. Did that mean Ford did? My stomach hurt just thinking about it. I wanted to be the one to explain the situation to him. He was going to be so hurt and betrayed.

"It has to be a shifter that killed Jensen," I insisted, my mind racing. "One of his own pack. He was going to inform on Jensen. He told me so. Besides, there's no way anyone else could've gotten close enough to do this without a fight."

Tanya Gellar, who had already crouched down next to Jensen's body, looked up at me, her expression serious. "That can't be, Hazel," she said, her voice clinical as she continued her examination. "This wound—" she pointed to the gaping, perfectly round hole in Jensen's chest "—it's been cauterized thoroughly. There's no blood, which means the blood vessels were staunched while the wound was created. That could only have been done with magic."

I stared at the charred hole in the werewolf's chest. The edges were smooth and charred, the scent of burnt flesh still lingering in the air. "Magic." I repeated, my mind struggling to connect the dots. "But shifters don't have that kind of power."

Tanya shook her head as she continued her assessment. "No, they don't. And that's what makes this so puzzling. His body is still warm. He's been dead less than an hour." She glanced at me pointedly. "Which matches the timeline the witness gave in her statement. Lividity has barely set in, and rigor mortis hasn't even started. Whoever did this knew exactly what they were doing, and they did it quickly."

The more Tanya spoke, the worse it sounded for me. All the evidence seemed to point in one horrifying direction: that magic had been involved, and in a way that only someone like me—or someone with my abilities—could have managed.

Then something struck me as odd. "Her?" I asked.

Tanya looked confused at my question.

"You said the witness gave *her* statement. It was a woman? Not a man?"

"I might've heard the officer who called me wrong."

"John!" I shouted.

Parker trotted over. "Chief?"

"Was the 9-1-1 caller a woman?"

"That's what dispatch said," he relayed. "Why?"

I'd assumed whoever had called me in the guise of a turncoat had been the same person to call the cops on me. My heart sank further. My setup was elaborate and calculated, but I couldn't understand why. Was the witch or warlock who killed Jensen the same one who brought him to town, and if that was the case, why would he or she kill their ace in the hole?

I was confident I knew the answer. This way, they removed Ford and me from the equation in one surgical strike.

"Two birds, one wolf," I murmured.

"What was that?" my dad asked.

I shook my head. "This is bad, Dad. Really freaking terrible."

Kent's grip on my shoulder tightened slightly, a silent reassurance. "You need to go home, Hazel," he said, echoing his mother's earlier command. His voice was gentle but firm, the protective tone of a father who didn't want to see his child hurt. "Let us handle this. I'll do everything I can to advocate on your behalf."

I nodded, my throat too tight to respond. At least my dad was on my side. That small bit of solidarity was the only thing keeping me from falling apart right there and then.

As I turned to leave, I noticed how some of my officers looked at me—or rather, how they avoided looking at me. Eyes that had once been filled with respect now glanced away, filled with doubt, fear, or worse...accusation. It was like a punch to the gut. I cursed myself silently for coming here alone, for making such a reckless decision that could cost me everything.

As I walked past them, my mind was already spinning, trying to figure out how I could prove that I hadn't killed Jensen and how I could make this right with Ford. How was I going to explain this to him? What would he say when I got home? Would he believe me? The uncertainty was unbearable, and the thought of seeing the same doubt in his eyes was almost too much to bear.

As I reached the edge of the clearing, I glanced back one last time. Jensen's body lay there, surrounded by my colleagues, while my grandmother and father worked to piece together a truth I already knew but couldn't prove. My stomach churned as I forced myself to keep walking.

I needed to be strong, to keep it together, for Ford, for Paradise Falls, and for myself. With each step, the weight on my shoulders grew heavier, and the path ahead seemed more uncertain than ever.

CHAPTER 11

MY HEART SANK as I spotted Ford through the front window, pacing back and forth. My guilt felt insurmountable, but I had to face the man I loved with all my heart. He was already dressed, car keys in hand. He'd been getting ready to come find me. The moment I stepped inside the house, his gaze locked onto mine, his expression a mix of worry and frustration.

"I didn't kill him," I said quickly.

"I know that," Ford replied.

"You do?" I blinked back the tears.

"Of course," he said, his voice calm but edged with a quiet intensity that told me just how upset he was. "I know you wouldn't stake someone to the ground on top of a pentagram to kill them. You'd just blast them and be done."

I forced a smile. "You know me so well."

"I thought I did." He kept his expression neutral. "Why didn't you tell me you were leaving?"

Again, guilt washed over me. I'd had the best intentions, but now, seeing the hurt in his eyes, I realized I'd made a terrible mistake by not telling him about the informant. "Ford, I'm sorry," I began, trying to find the right words. "I was following up on a call I got earlier today."

"Earlier?" His gaze narrowed. "Before or after you came over to the courthouse?"

Well, this was going as badly as I thought it would. "Uhm, before," I replied tentatively. Then rapid-fire added, "But the caller had said he was part of Jensen's pack, and he said that he had proof that Jensen was up to no good and planned to cheat at the challenge. He also said that if I brought anyone, he'd leave and take his evidence on Jensen with him. I couldn't risk losing that chance. I worried that if you knew, you wouldn't let me go alone, and I was desperate to take Jensen down so you wouldn't have to fight him to the death. So when he texted an hour and a half ago, I had to go and meet him. You see that, right?" My excuses sounded weak and pathetic even to my own ears, considering the outcome, but they were the only defense I had at the moment.

Ford stood still, his jaw clenched. His calm exterior didn't waver, but the emotion in his tone was unmistakable. "I'm disappointed, Hazel. Not just because you didn't tell me where you were going but because you didn't trust me enough to fight my battles. And because you felt like you had to keep secrets from me."

I nodded, feeling the sting of his words cut deep. He was right. I had control issues, and I knew it. I always felt like if I wasn't the one fixing things, they wouldn't get fixed. It was a survival instinct born from years of only having myself to rely on. But I wasn't alone anymore. Ford had been by my side for a while now, and I needed to start trusting him as much as he trusted me. Or at least as much as he trusted me before I went and got myself set up for the murder of an alpha werewolf.

"You're right," I admitted softly. "And I do trust you. It's not that, and I think you know it. It's just that, for too many years, I conditioned myself to be tenaciously self-reliant, and it's a hard habit to break. It makes me a good investigator but a terrible mate. I'm so very sorry. More than I can express. But, honestly, I know I'm not alone anymore. You're here, and I can always rely on you. I promise I'll be better, and I hope you forgive me."

Ford's expression softened, and he stepped closer, wrapping his arms around me. "You're not alone, Hazel. You don't have to carry everything by yourself. I'm here, and we're in this together."

I leaned into him, letting the warmth of his

embrace calm the storm inside me. Breathing suddenly felt easier. After a moment, I pulled back slightly to look up at him. "There's more," I said, my voice steadying as I prepared to tell him about the scene at the park. "My grandmother showed up. She's taking over the investigation, and my dad said the Witch-Shifter Coalition will probably convene a public hearing to review whether I'm fit to continue as chief while this plays out."

Ford's eyes darkened with concern. "Did you show the Grand Inquisitor the text message?"

"I lost my phone when I poofed over to the lake."

"Oh, Hazel," he said gently. "I'll search for it on the Find-My-Family app."

"I forgot you had that." I gave his chest a pat. "Good thinking."

"I've been known to have a good idea or two." He took his phone from the holder on his belt.

"And Tanya," I continued, while he looked for my cell phone, "she said there was a witness. A female witness who identified me as the killer. Which is impossible, of course, because I didn't do it."

Ford's brow furrowed, and he was momentarily silent, processing everything I'd just told him. Then he spoke. "Got it. It's still active."

"Where is it?"

"It's in a three-hundred-yard radius near the lake,

but the good news is that I'm getting a signal, so it's not underwater."

"Bad news," I said. "We can't get it right now because the place is crawling with cops and civilian gawkers, maybe even a reporter or two."

"Well..." Ford's brows raised. "I'm not short on ideas. You remember Tizzy's comment about the junkyard? She mentioned that the garage there has been warded by magic to keep prying eyes out. That seems like something worth checking out, don't you think? And I have a feeling the pack is going to be otherwise occupied this morning, seeing as how their alpha is dead."

I raised an eyebrow, intrigued. Ford had been a great cop before becoming mayor, and his instincts were razor-sharp. "Yeah, that is true," I said, the wheels in my mind turning. "Why not? Until the coalition says otherwise, I'm still the police chief. And investigating the strange goings-on of the pack isn't exactly the same as investigating the alpha's murder, right?"

A small smile tugged at Ford's lips, the kind of smile that reminded me just how much he enjoyed being on the job. "Right," he agreed. "Not the same at all."

I couldn't help but smile back at him. Ford might be the mayor now, but he was still a cop at heart. The Grand Inquisitor had stood me down, but technically investigating the junkyard wasn't going against her orders. Besides, I wasn't about to sit around and do nothing while my career and life hung in the balance.

It was five in the morning, and I'd had next to zero sleep, but having a purpose energized me. "I'm ready to go now if you are," I said. "I'm sure the pack has heard about Jensen by now and have cleared out."

"Maybe you ought to change your shoes first." He glanced down at my feet. "Don't want you getting toe-rot."

"My feet." I checked out my sneakers, and when I saw the damp floor, I realized that they were still wet with lake water. I'd been so numb on the short walk home that I'd forgotten. I'm sure my piggies were wrinkled raisins at this point. "Right." I gave him a quick salute. "First, change shoes. Second, pack heat." I was taking my gun and a couple of knives for good measure.

Ford grinned. "Sounds like a plan."

Was it a good plan? Probably not, but at least we weren't sitting around twiddling our thumbs while our fates were decided for us.

Ford and I parked in a clearing of trees about a half mile from the Junkyard Dog. The dense foliage provided good cover, but we weren't taking any chances. We slipped into the woods, moving carefully to avoid being seen. The August terrain was overgrown and uneven, forcing us to dodge roots and low-hanging branches. The darkness of the early morning added to the tension, every rustle of leaves or snap of a twig making me second-guess our path.

When we reached a flat clearing, I paused. Beyond us lay the open field that stretched out to the garage. The field was a trap in the making, a wide-open space where any misstep would expose us. I took a deep breath and whispered a spell I'd been working on for stakeouts, one that would make us harder to detect. The effectiveness of it had been hit or miss, but I prayed to the Goddess that this time it would work.

"Goddess cloak our way,

Make our steps like shadow play.

Let us pass unseen, unheard,

As silent as a whisper, as light as a bird.

Grant us cover, keep us free,

From prying eyes, so mote it be."

As the final words left my lips, I felt the familiar tingle of magic settle over me. I looked at Ford. "Fingers crossed," I said.

We continued, creeping closer to the Junkyard

Dog. As we approached, it became clear that the werewolves had turned the property into Tent City. Makeshift shelters were scattered around, forming a temporary encampment. The information Sarah, my FBI contact, had shared made sense now. Jensen and his pack were nomadic, always on the move, causing trouble from town to town. This was just another stop on their malevolent journey.

Ford tilted his head slightly, his shifter hearing picking up on sounds beyond my witch range. "I think everyone's gone," he whispered, his voice low and certain. "I don't hear anything."

I nodded, trusting his instincts. We moved forward, finally reaching the garage. I could feel the barrier magic before we even got close. It buzzed against my skin, a subtle but unmistakable force. Tizzy had warned me about this. She hadn't been able to apparate inside the structure, which meant the magic was strong, likely designed to keep out prying eyes. After my earlier translocation mishap that landed me in the lake, I wasn't about to try anything fancy. We'd do this the old-fashioned way, through the door.

Ford and I exchanged a glance, then approached the front of the garage. I was surprised to find it was not only unguarded but also unlocked. It creaked open, revealing the interior of the garage. There was a car lift in the corner where I'd first investigated

Danny Mason's car after his death. There was a large arc welder, and toolboxes and cabinets lined the walls. The place had been cleaned of dust and rust. But that wasn't what surprised me. There was something in the garage that definitely didn't belong there.

In the center of the room stood a twisted, gnarled tree. It was smaller than the one I'd seen before, but its resemblance was unmistakable. My stomach churned at the sight. It was just like the tree my best friend Lily Mason had been tied to when Adele Abbot had captured and tortured her. The memory was vivid, and the vile power that seeped from that tree was unforgettable.

But this tree had a new victim.

Dick, Jensen's beta, was bound to the trunk, his condition far worse than Lily's had been. His arms and legs had melded with the tree, and his blood dribbled down the cracks of the bark, making it look as if the tree was bleeding. The back of his head was also fused into the wood.

"Is he dead?" I whispered.

Ford shook his head. "Breathing," he said quietly. "But just barely."

No one jumped out from any hiding places to attack us, so we made our way across the garage to the tree.

"Dick," I hissed when we were standing in front

of him. This close, I could hear his shallow, labored breaths.

The werewolf blinked as if just now seeing me. My stealth spell must've worked. He managed to rasp out two words, "Kill me."

Ford and I exchanged a quick, horrified look. This was just like what Adele and her cult had done to the shifters they'd tortured and killed to gain power. But why Dick? He was part of the pack, so why were they treating him like a lamb to the slaughter? Had Jensen put him on the tree as some twisted punishment? Or had the person who killed Jensen done this?

"Who did this to you?" I demanded.

"She haaaaasss plansss," he moaned. "Worse...than...this. Sooo muuuch paain. Please kill...kiiilll..." His voice faded off as he passed out from the pain.

"We can't leave him there," Ford said, his voice steady despite the tension in the air. "I don't care who or what he belongs to. This is wrong."

"Evil," I said. "Pure evil." He was right. No matter what group Dick had arrived with, he was still a person and didn't deserve to be tortured like this.

I reached for the knife I'd strapped to my leg. With my first dig into the bark near his head, the tree began to pulse with malevolence, feasting on

Dick and drawing him in. The werewolf roused from unconsciousness and cried out in pain. Every cut made it worse. I stopped trying. "We're killing him," I told Ford. Only we were giving him a much slower death than he'd asked for. "I don't know what to do. I'm not sure we can save him."

My husband growled his frustration.

"I...am bait," Dick ground out.

"Bait? Bait for who?"

His eyes widened, his gray eyes flashing amber. "For you," he said. "Wonder..." He gasped a breath.

"Wonder what?" I asked. "What do you wonder?"

"Wond..." He didn't finish as the light of life was snuffed from him. His mouth gaped open, and the tree's hold on his skull was the only thing keeping his chin from dropping to his chest.

Ford and I looked at each other.

"Did he say Bait?" Ford's brow dipped. "What do you think he meant by 'for you'?"

"I don't know." It didn't take long to find out.

The door to the garage flung open, and the Grand Inquisitor, along with several of my officers, walked in. My grandmother let out a string of colorful expletives, then said, "Hazel Kinsey and Ford Baylor, you will be held for the suspicious death of Brahm Jensen..." Her face soured. "And whoever this unfortunate gentleman is. And you will be held until the investigation has concluded. Depending on our findings, you will either be arrested or released at that time."

"You've got to be freaking kidding me," I seethed. "You're taking me in?"

"You can stay in the cells at your station, or you can be transported to my jail." She crossed her arms over her chest. "Your call."

"Can Ford and I share a cell?" I asked.

My grandmother nodded.

"Fine, then I choose here."

Ford leaned in and asked, "Why am I being held?"

The Grand Inquisitor's voice grew loud and booming, her words flooded with intimidating power. "Because you're as bad as my granddaughter. When I tell you to stand down and let me handle a situation, that's exactly what I expect you to do."

Ford grimaced.

We had walked into a trap. One that I should've seen coming. I don't know how the bad guys or gals had figured out we'd go here, but it seemed apparent now that getting inside had been easy. A little too easy. Everything was spiraling more out of control, and stopping it from a jail cell would be no easy feat. I slipped my hand into Ford's. "I'll figure this out," I told him. "I'll make this right."

He gave the barest of a headshake, then said, "We'll figure this out. We'll make it right."

"We." I squeezed his hand and turned into his arms. "I love you."

"I love you."

"Oh, for Goddess's sake," Tizzy squawked as she suddenly appeared on my shoulder. "You moon-eyed idiots need to get ready to go."

"Go where?" Ford asked.

"Hold on to Grizzly Adams," she told him. "You're about to go on a ride."

Next thing I knew, my father poofed in next to us.

"What the...?" I asked as Dad wrapped his arms around Ford and me. I heard my grandmother bellow his name before, in a blink, he transported us out of there.

CHAPTER 12

I LOOKED around the palatial living space. It was open concept, kitchen, dining, and living room all in one large area. Floor-to-ceiling sliding glass doors on the back wall opened to a grand deck overlooking a mountain range.

I let go of Ford, who appeared as stunned as I was, then turned to my dad. "What is this place?"

"It's my safe house," he replied.

"You have a safe house?" Ford asked.

Then I added, "Why in the world do you need a safe house?"

His expression was pure exasperation. "Live in witch jail for seventeen years for a crime you didn't commit and then tell me you wouldn't get a safe house somewhere no one could find you."

He had a point. "Fine." I threw up my hands. "But what are we supposed to do now? We can't stay here, Dad. Paradise Falls is in real danger, and if we don't catch whoever's pulling the puppet strings, then our friends and family are going to suffer for it."

"You would've rather been in jail?" he asked.

"At least if we were in a cell at our station, I could coordinate my officers' investigations."

"Bah!" He threw up his hands. "Your officers turned on you the minute things looked bad. You can't count on them."

What went down at the park had made me look bad, and I could understand the officers under me might be suspicious, even so, none of them had been hostile, nor had they made a move to arrest. "I have loyal cops on my team, and I know I could talk the others around."

"Bah!" he said again.

"Stop that," I told him. I realized one of our crew hadn't made it. "Where's Tiz?"

"She's our eyes and ears back home." He tapped his nose.

"You have to stop watching spy movies," I told him.

Ford had made his way to the sliding glass doors and was staring out at the view. "Where are we?"

"Colorado," my dad replied.

My mate sighed. "It's breathtaking."

"Don't get used to it," I said. "We're not staying." I turned my attention back to Dad. The man had risked his freedom, however misguided, to save me. I couldn't be mad at him. Instead, I did something rare and wonderful. I hugged him. "Thank you, Dad."

"You're welcome, but just for clarity," he queried, "you were yelling at me a second ago, so what are you thanking me for now?"

"For loving me."

"Oh." His voice cracked before he began to bluster, "Uhm, it's my, uh, pleasure. Well, you know what I mean."

"I do." I hugged him tighter. "I love you too." Who had emotional walls? Not this girl. Not anymore. "Now, take us back to Paradise Falls."

"What will that solve?"

"I have proof that I was set up," I informed him. "Or at least strong evidence."

Now my father got interested. "What proof?"

"I have the text message from the informant telling me to meet him. It's time-stamped, so that should be enough to at least give me reasonable doubt."

My dad's eyes narrowed. "Why didn't you say that to the old battleaxe this morning?"

"Because she wouldn't let me." I shrugged. "I was going to tell her about it when she came to get my statement."

"Why tell? Why not show?"

I frowned. "I lost it during my translocation spell to the lake."

His expression was pure befuddlement. "So, it could be in the lake?"

Ford took out his phone. "No reception up here but my phone is trying to connect to Kent's Wireless." He looked at my dad. "What's your wifi password?"

"Hazel's Dad. All one word. No caps."

"You're kidding?" I asked him as my heart squeezed in my chest.

"It works," Ford said. "Thanks, Kent."

My dad had used me as his password. I think it might've been the sweetest thing ever.

"Phone's still active," Ford told us. "My Find-My-Family app shows it hasn't moved since the last time I tracked it. It's still in the general area of the lake. As long as the battery holds out, we should be able to find it."

"See?" I beamed a smile at my father. "Everything is going to be fine."

"But I helped you escape. I took you on the lamb." Panic crossed Dad's face. "I'm going back to jail. She's going to lock me up and throw away the key this time. And it was all for nothing."

"Not nothing." I patted his face. "Now I know for sure that you love me more than anyone else."

"My dear daughter." The corner of his eyes gentled. "I didn't realize you had any doubts."

"Not anymore." I smiled. "Can we go back now?"

He nodded. "Come over here, Ford."

"Damn," my bear said. "This is the closest thing I've ever had to a real vacation. I can't even remember the last time I left the county, let alone the state."

That made me sad. When we got through this mess, I was going to make a point to take my man somewhere gorgeous and secluded. Just the two of us.

"Hold on," Dad ordered.

We held, and in another blink, we were at Paradise Falls Police Station, and standing in front of the old battleaxe herself.

I grimaced. "Surprise."

The moment we materialized back at the Paradise Falls Police Station, I found myself staring into the stern, flawless face of the Grand Inquisitor. She stood there, hands on her hips, her eyes narrowing as she took in the sight of us.

The station buzzed with low murmurs as officers caught sight of us, but they quickly looked away, pretending to focus on their tasks. Some of them threw sympathetic glances my way, while others were more cautious, their expressions betraying their wariness. But none of them dared to openly challenge me. Respectful or fearful? I wasn't sure. Maybe a bit of both.

"Kent Kinsey," Clementine began, her voice carrying the kind of weight that made grown men tremble. "What in the Goddess's name were you thinking, whisking Hazel away like that? Do you have any idea what kind of mess you've made?"

Dad winced but held his ground. "I was trying to protect my daughter, mother. Some parents actually care about their children."

I could see his words struck his mom the way he'd intended.

"It's not an excuse to break witch law."

"I can't personally think of a better one," he countered. "Family first in my family."

I was worried if Dad kept this up, my grand-mother would put him in jail just to shut him up. "He wasn't helping me escape," I interjected. "He didn't want to see me humiliated by having my own officers haul me into the station. It was always his plan to bring Ford and me here." I widened my eyes at my father. "Isn't that right, Dad?"

He looked like a swallowed a toad.

"Is that true, Kent?" his mother asked.

My dad bristled, then said, "Yes," without any elaboration.

The battleaxe's eyes flicked to me, then back to Dad, her expression a mix of exasperation and something that looked a little like pity. "You could have made things worse for Hazel, Kent. Interfering in an ongoing investigation. If you hadn't brought her here, I would be tracking you down to your little vacation home in the Rockies right now and taking you back to prison." She straightened her jacket. "But you did bring her back, so I'm going to let it slide."

"How very generous," he uttered. The man was begging for trouble.

Stepping forward, I put a hand on Dad's arm, gently pulling him back. "He was trying to help, Grandma. It might've been misguided, but it was earnest. You don't have to punish him." I gave my dad a quick hug. "I appreciate what you've done, but you should get while the getting is good."

Clementine looked at me, her gaze sharp as ever, but I saw the tiniest flicker of concern in her eyes. "Hazel, if you wanted to clear your name, running off wasn't the way to do it. I have to appear impartial or the board of high witches will lose confidence in my ability to handle my job. If that happens, there will be nothing I can do for you."

"I didn't run off." I took a deep breath, trying to keep my voice steady. "I was dragged off by a well-meaning but overzealous father."

Ford put his arm around me. A show of solidarity. "We're here now, and we're cooperating. No harm done."

"And I have proof," I told her. "There's a text message from an informant telling me to go to the park. It's time-stamped. That should at least be enough to raise reasonable doubt."

"Why didn't you tell me sooner?" Clementine's gaze narrowed.

It didn't seem productive to point out that she hadn't let me tell her jack crap at the lake. "I'm telling you now."

"Where's the phone?" she asked.

I cringed a little. "I, uh, lost it during my translocation mishap into the lake. But Ford has a 'find my family' app on his phone. It can be tracked."

Ford nodded and pulled out his phone, showing the app's screen. "It's still active. If you do a ground search in this area in front of the lake, you should be able to find it, no problem."

"We can call it when we get there, right?" she asked.

I shook my head. "It was on vibrate."

"Terrific." Clementine sighed, rubbing her temples as if trying to stave off a headache. "Hazel, I'm afraid I will have to ask you and Ford to sit tight in one of the magic-proof cells until I can figure out what the hell is going on."

I started to protest, but she held up a hand.

"Don't argue, granddaughter. I'm in no mood. Besides, you're too close to this. Let me handle the investigation into Jensen's death and whatever happened at that garage. You'll get your chance to clear your name, but right now, I need to ensure nothing else goes wrong."

Bex came over when the Grand Inquisitor gestured for her. "Take these two down and get them comfortable."

"Yes, ma'am," Bex said sharply. She gave me a sweet, apologetic smile. "Sorry about this, chief. No one wanted the job of putting you in the cell, and I drew the short straw."

As she escorted us to the holding cells, I said, "No one, huh? How come?" I figured a few of them, like John Parker would be chomping at the bit to take me down a notch.

"Most of them know you're innocent, Chief, and anyone who has doubts, thinks you were justified." She put a comforting hand on my shoulder as she ushered us into the first cell. "We're your people, and we're on your side."

Emotion swelled in me and I fought not to tear up. "Thanks, Bex."

She nodded. "Can I get you any coffee? A pastry?"

"Make it two of each," Ford told her.

"Coming right up," Bex said with a wink.

"That's a good girl, there," Ford said. "Lincoln is a dumbass if he doesn't come back and marry her."

Lincoln was Ford's brother. He and Bex had caught each other's scents their senior year, but Lincoln had gone off to college to study engineering, and Bex had stayed behind. I only hoped they didn't wait seventeen years to find each other again like I had with Ford.

"She really is," I told him. I couldn't stop the grin spreading on my face. My heart raced fast and I saw a light at the end of a very dark tunnel. Bex truly had my back as much as I had hers.

"Why are you smiling like that?" my husband asked nervously.

"Because this cell is not magic proof."

His eyes widened. "Bex made a mistake?"

I shook my head. My smile was now so wide, my cheeks hurt. "I haven't seen that girl make a mistake since I hired her."

"So, we can basically come and go as we please."

I nodded. "Yep, we sure can."

"Then we're still in this investigation."

"We were never out," I told him.

To paraphrase Sherlock Holmes, the game was on like Donkey Kong, or something to that effect. My officers hadn't lost faith in me. They were loyal, and when this was over, I planned to repay their trust in spades.

CHAPTER 13

THE COFFEE WAS HOT, and the pastries were sweet, but I was already feeling claustrophobic and anxious to be out of the cell. "I love you, Ford, but I'm not sure this tiny room is big enough for the two of us." I glanced at the urinal and toilet against the far wall and put my coffee down. "I'll be damned if I'm using the bathroom here. When we get out of this, I'm requisitioning curtains. This is inhumane."

"You're just now realizing that jail isn't a picnic?"

"I knew it was bad, but seeing it from this perspective drives home just how awful it is."

Tizzy scampered across the floor and shoved herself through the bars. "You've been here less than an hour, Hazel. I don't think you can count that as hard time."

"Tiz!" I was more excited to see her than I

RENEE GEORGE

wanted to admit. In other words, I was bored out of my skull. "There's nothing to do in jail."

"Because it's not the YMCA," she said. "I'd ask how you're holding up, but you've already answered."

"Dad said you were going to be our eyes and ears here. What have you learned so far?"

"Well..." Her cheeks puffed up, and her brown eyes grew watery with tears.

My heart clenched. "It's okay, Tiz. We'll get out of this somehow. Keep the faith."

"It's not that," she squeaked. "Lupita is cheating on me."

"No," I hissed. "She wouldn't dare." I mean, I didn't like the cat, but I'd never doubted her love for Tizzy. They'd formed a bond so strong that at one point, she'd become my familiar's familiar.

"She dares," Tiz said. "She dares in the extreme."

"How do you know?"

Her little squirrel lips quivered. "She's been disappearing all the time. Gone for hours. When she comes home, she always has a lame excuse, like Book Club. Book Club!" she reiterated.

"Book Club sounds reasonable."

Tiz stared daggers at me. "Lupita hates reading."

"Okay." I waved my hand in a flourish. "Do go on."

"I followed her last night, and I saw her meet

Spike outside the community center building. They looked real damn cozy."

"Spike?"

"Darwin Brewer's tomcat familiar," she fairly spat. "A tomcat! Not only is Lupita cheating on me, but she's cheating on me with a dude." Tiz started crying.

Then I started crying. "Come here." I held out my arms to her, and she jumped onto my lap for a cuddle. "I'm so sorry, Tiz. You deserve better than this."

"Damn straight," Ford agreed. "If she doesn't cherish you, then she's a fool."

His words of comfort made her cry harder. "Don't be nice to me, Baloo. I couldn't take it if I had to stop tormenting you."

He chuckled. "You got it, Rocky."

"Awww," I cooed, and in my best fake Russian accent, said, "Moose loves Squirrel."

"Can I move back in with you?" Tiz sniffled.

"Of course, you can," I told her. "My home is your home. Always."

I heard the soft patter of boots coming down the hall. Bex was almost breathless as she got to the cell. "Chief, bad news."

"You couldn't find my cell phone?"

"We're still looking," she said. "That's not the bad news."

"Spit it out, Bex."

"A Beastmaster has arrived in town."

Ford stood up. "Are you sure?"

"That's what he says." Her eyes were wide. "He's over seven feet tall and makes Ford look like a little guy." She shook her head. "I guess the werewolves called him. They want a judgment on the Rite of Arphilitian and don't want to wait on the Grand Inquisitor's investigation."

"Pixie on a stick," Tiz swore. "How much time does Ford have to make his case?"

Oh, Goddess. I forgot Ford was the one who would take the hit from the Beastmaster, not me. "That's not fair. He can't come after Ford until I've been proven guilty. What kind of justice is that?"

"The shifter kind," Ford said quietly. He scratched his short beard. "It's okay."

"It's not." The pit of my stomach burned. "How much time, Bex?"

"The Beastmaster wants to hold a trial today in front of all the shifter factions here in Paradise Falls. Those under Mr. Baylor, Ms. Lowe, and Mr. Crandell. Jensen's pack as the challengers will be there as well." Bex nervously bit the side of her thumbnail. "They've made it an open trial, so the witches and warlocks in town can attend. From what I'm hearing, it's going to be a full house."

"Well, crap." I met Ford's gaze. "This is going to get ugly."

"We have right on our side," he said.

I loved my mate with every fiber of my being, but sometimes he could be naive. "I know from personal experience that doesn't always matter."

Ford shook his head. "We'll make it matter."

"Where is the trial taking place?" I asked Bex.

"The community center. It's the only building big enough to handle the entire town. They are pulling out bleachers and setting up chairs on the gym floor." She cringed. "It's going to be a spectacle." She tapped a bar on the cell. "You know, unless you all weren't here."

"I'm not running," Ford stated. "If I do that, I'll forfeit the town to these jackals."

"But I don't have to stay."

"Explain," he said.

"I could 'escape' and go search for evidence to clear your name and mine. Since the Beastmaster isn't waiting for a summary judgment against me, it sounds like my incarceration makes zero difference to the outcome of your trial. The only way we're going to save you and the town is by providing concrete proof that not only did I not kill that alpha piece of crap, but that he wasn't on the level with the whole challenge in the first place. The key is finding the witch responsible for bringing his stupid ass here in the first place."

Ford's eyes darkened. "Where would you even start?"

"Golda Gedes," I said. "Our local historian knows something. She was holding back when we interviewed her yesterday, and I think if I talk to her alone, I could get her to spill the beans."

Bex nodded like it was a good idea, but she looked as if she wanted to puke. "How will you get around without being seen? And it'll be obvious you're not in the cell when they come to get Ford?"

The familiar click-clack of heels told me who our next guest was. "It's Tanya," I told them. "We can trust her." She might not always love me, but she loved my dad and would never do anything to hurt him.

"Hazel." Her strawberry-blonde hair had perfect coiled curls, beautiful and shiny. "Your dad told me to tell you you need to get out now."

"That's the goal," I said. "The problem is, once I'm gone, it's going to be pretty obvious."

"That's why I'm here." She looked rather pleased with herself. "I'm going to give you a little help in that department."

"You are?" Color me surprised. "How?"

"By swapping places with you."

I narrowed my gaze at her. "We don't exactly look

alike." She was way more put together than I was, and my hair was super light blonde and straight as a rod.

"You're in luck." She waved her perfectly manicured nails in front of me. "A little known fact." She shook her hand, and her nail color changed, but it wasn't just the nail color; it was also the shape of her hands. Her fingers had become shorter, her palm more square. She shook her hand again, and the nail color and hand shape changed once more.

"Cool trick," I told her. "I bet it won you a lot of beers in college, but I'm not sure how being able to change your nails and hands is going to help."

She let out an exasperated sigh. "It's not just hands that I can change." She whispered the next part. "I can change the way I look from head to toe. I can do it on other people as well."

"Seriously?" I gave Tanya a quick assessment. I'd never really seen her use much magic, just doctor stuff. I guess I'd always thought she didn't have much power. I looked at Ford. He and Tanya had been friends in high school. She had been his ex-girlfriend's bestie. "Did you know she could do that?"

He shook his head. "Not a clue."

Tanya said, "No one knows." She raised her hands, palms up. "Unless you count my mom. Oh, and Kent, of course. I don't keep secrets from him."

"Why in the world would you keep this a secret? What a cool freaking power," Bex exclaimed.

Tanya sighed again. "Because I have a reputation as an attractive, stylish witch. If people were to discover that my power gave me the ability to change my looks, then everyone would always wonder if I was actually beautiful or if it was an illusion." She narrowed her gaze at me. "And before you ask, this is how I look." She jerked her shoulders. "Maybe I help the hair, but everything else is one hundred percent au natural."

"So, you can make me look like you, and you look like me," I summed up.

"That's the gist of it."

"This is too much like an episode of the Twilight Zone," Tiz said. "Too weird for words."

"Do you want my help or not?" Tanya asked. "Offer ends in four, three, two..."

"I accept," I told her before she got to one. I looked at Ford. "Is that all right with you?"

He nodded. "It's a shot."

Bex opened the door to the cell, and Tanya walked inside. She quietly incanted a spell, and in seconds, she looked like my mirror image. Only, when I looked down at my hands, they weren't my short, but clean fingernails—they were her long, ornately painted talons.

"This is sooooo creepy," Tiz whispered. "It's

Hazel, but not Hazel, and damn, Hazel, you look just like Tanya, down to her snooty scowl."

My husband was staring at me like I'd grown a third head. "Well?"

"You'll pass for Tanya." He glanced at Tanya. "You're very good."

She happily preened at the compliment. I looked at her hair. "Hey, how'd you get my hair so silky looking?"

She smiled. "Magic."

Her voice still sounded like her, and I guessed that I sounded like me. "We'll have to keep the chat to a minimum. Don't want anyone recognizing us from the way we speak."

Tanya nodded. "I don't want to be in here all day, so do what you have to do, then get me out of here."

I tipped my head to her. "You got it." Next, I grabbed Ford by the shirt and pulled him close. "Just remember, mister. She might look like me, but she's not me."

"She may look like you, but no one has your scent, Hazel Kinsey. I would know you if you looked like a cow."

"I can do that too," Tanya crooned.

"I'm good," I told her without looking away from Ford. "Please watch yourself today. I have a feeling that if it looks like you are winning, whoever's behind this will have a contingency."

He pressed his forehead to mine, and I was never so glad he didn't go for the kiss. I didn't care if it was me on the inside. I didn't want my husband kissing Tanya's lips.

"Love you," I said.

"Love you more," he said back.

"Not possible."

"Okaaaay," Tizzy said. "Waaaaay too weird. Let's go while the getting's good."

As I was leaving, I hugged Tanya. At first, she was stiff in my arms, but after a second, she relaxed and hugged me back. "Thank you," I told her. "Thank you so much."

"My pleasure," she replied, a little stunned. "I thought I was doing this for Kent, but now, I'm not so sure."

Strange thing was, I knew she meant it. Tanya and I had moved from enemies, to frenemies, to friends, and finally, we'd become family.

"Keep the faith," I told Ford. "I'll find the proof to clear us, even if I have to zap someone to get it."

His eyes widened.

I smiled. "It was a joke."

As I slipped out of the jail, disguised in Tanya's flawless illusion, I was more determined than ever to find the witch behind the wolves.

CHAPTER 14

DRIVING Tanya's fancy Mercedes-Benz made me nervous. I was used to something more rugged, a vehicle that could take a beating. The only thing that would take a beating if I damaged Tanya's car was my bank account. I had left the police station with the intent to talk to Golda first, but when I drove past Pierce Roberts' office, I decided to speak with him instead. His conversation with Sally Teeter might've been nothing, but it might've been something. If he was interested in the property adjoining the junkyard, I wanted to know why. With everything happening, it seemed suspicious. I parked the car next to the curb and got out.

Pierce Roberts, a thin man with sandy-blond hair and deep-set green eyes, was sitting in his office behind his cherry wood desk. He had a book open and was leafing through the pages. The pale blue walls with forest green accents gave the room a vibrancy I wouldn't have expected from a man like Pierce. He had plants in his windows, giving his place of business a comfortable warmth. I'd never really thought about what magic he was good at, but maybe it was plants. His were always thriving, no matter the season. It seemed to me that someone good with house plants might also be skilled with trees. Big, nasty gnarly ones.

He looked up at me when I walked in, and I expected his normal scowl. Instead, he flashed me a bright, genial smile. "Tanya, so good to see you." He got up and shook my hand. "Did we have an appointment? Not that I mind you stopping by without one. It's always so nice to see you."

I nearly choked. In all the time I knew Pierce, the man had never even said hello. I thought he was probably an asshole to everyone. But nope, it was just me.

I tried to make my voice a little higher to match Tanya's—or at the very least, not sound like me. "I'm out running errands, and I saw you through the window. Just thought I would say hi."

"Lovely," he said, though he was giving me a funny look. "Is there something wrong with your throat?"

"Woke up with a frog in there." I made a ribbit sound.

He laughed. "You are a delight."

I struggled to stop my face from reflecting the many emotions and thoughts running through my head. "So," I said nonchalantly, "Terrible business with these werewolves in town."

"It's disgusting," Pierce replied. "I know you're with Kent, and he's a good man, but his daughter is a scourge on this town."

I coughed to cover my surprise. "She's not so bad," I told him. "She cares about the town. That has to count for something."

"I know it's not PC to say this these days, but as far as I'm concerned, a witch who mixes with a shifter is borrowing trouble."

Whoa, I thought. Racist much? The fact that he was comfortable saying this crap to Tanya concerned me as well. Her best friend in high school had been a bear shifter. On top of that, she'd tried to date Ford before I returned to town.

"She's a good person, and so is her husband," I chastised him.

"Oh, don't mind me," he said, as if finally reading the room. "I don't mean anything by it. Some of my best friends are shifters."

Said every bigot ever. Ugh. I really, really,

reeeaaaallllly hoped this guy was guilty. I would love to lock him up and throw away the key. "So, I, uh, hear you're looking to buy some property outside of town."

His gaze grew shrewd. "Where'd you hear that?"

"A patient who was at a restaurant a day or two ago said that they overheard you talking to Sally Teeter about it."

He eyeballed me suspiciously as he closed his book. "Why do you care?"

"Oh." I shook my head. "I am looking to invest some money, and I thought you were looking at the property for commercial reasons." I tried to make my smile flirty as I softened my tone. "You're just so good with money."

He relaxed in his high-back leather chair. Apparently, all I had to do was stroke his ego, and he was willing to believe whatever BS I told him.

"I wanted to find out who bought Adele Abbot's old farm outside of town. I thought if I bought it, I could prevent the werewolves from taking up any more territory outside our town. Once that type gets a toehold, it's only a matter of time before they start moving into town."

I remembered Steve Crandell had said something similar at the Witch-Shifter Coalition meeting. Was that the "some of my best friends" Pierce had been talking about? Possibly. Did it matter? Probably not.

Pierce was just a small-minded, unpleasant warlock. Even so, I had to ask, "Did you nurture all these plants yourself? They are beautiful."

His cheeks reddened as he puffed his chest with pride. "Every single one of them." He pointed to a fern on the far right. "I've had Frannie for eighty-nine years."

"Wow. That's impressive." I meant it. I could barely keep a plant alive for a couple of weeks. He'd managed to keep his alive for nearly a century. "What's your secret?"

"I've always had a gift for the green."

"Even trees?"

"Yes," he said. "But I'm not really an outdoor type."

I faked a Tanya giggle. "You're so funny." Ugh. Gag me now.

Pierce grinned. "I'm here all day, five days a week, folks."

His answers had seemed honest. The man was awful, but he didn't feel like a liar. I tried to think of something Tanya would say in farewell and settled on, "Thanks for the chit-chat. Toodaloo."

"Toodaloo," he called after me as I exited the office back to the street.

After leaving Pierce's office, I headed straight to Golda's house. The conversation with Pierce had left a bitter taste in my mouth, and it had been unproductive. Golda, on the other hand, knew more than she was letting on. If I had to pry it out of her, so be it.

When I arrived at Golda's, she greeted me at the door, her sharp eyes narrowing as she took in my appearance. "Tanya, now's not a good time," she said, her voice tense. "Can you come back later?"

Golda and Tanya were on the Witch-Shifter Coalition together, so I knew she'd be more likely to talk to her, or at least who she thought was her. I pressed on. "Golda, as the witch representatives in town, we need to talk about what's happening with Ford's trial at the community center. It can't wait."

Golda's eyes narrowed further, suspicion dawning on her face. "You're not Tanya, are you?" she said, her voice low and wary. "Hazel?"

I sighed, dropping the pretense. "Yes, it's me. We need to talk, and I won't take no for an answer."

Golda hesitated for a moment, then nodded curtly. "Give me a minute." She disappeared into the house, closing the door between us. I waited, tension building in my chest, until she returned and gestured for me to enter.

We moved to the sitting room, and I cut to the chase. "What were you hiding when we talked yesterday? I know you know more about Adele

Abbot, and I have every right to know if it could affect the outcome of Ford's trial."

Golda's expression darkened. "Some secrets are the kind you should take to your grave. Broken promises cause the most damage."

Her words were vague, frustratingly so. I leaned forward. "What secrets, Golda? What promises?"

Before she could answer, the burner phone Bex had given me buzzed in my pocket. I pulled it out and read the message. Ford was being transported to the community center. The trial would commence in an hour.

Desperation clawed at me. "Golda, I need the truth. Now."

"Or what?" she asked, her voice cold. "You'll burn a hole through me as well?"

The statement hit me like a slap in the face. "I didn't kill that werewolf."

"That's not what I've been told. A witness has come forward with the truth."

I felt the blood drain from my face. "Are you that witness?" I asked, my voice barely above a whisper. "Are you the person who brought the Arete back to town?"

Golda's eyes widened in shock, genuine dismay etched into her features. "Of course not," she said, her voice trembling slightly. "I would never do anything to destroy this town. And no, the witness isn't me."

As she spoke, my gaze drifted to a picture hanging on the wall. It showed Golda with her arm around Sally Teeter, who was wearing a cap and gown. "Do you know Sally well?" I asked, pointing to the frame.

Golda flinched, a slight, almost imperceptible movement. "Why are you asking about Sally?"

"It looks like you're close," I said.

"I looked out for her, is all," Golda replied, her voice tight. "She had a rough time with her parents when she was young."

Her parents, huh? It dawned on me that one of the missing records at the courthouse had been a sealed adoption file. I narrowed my gaze on Golda. She'd never married. As far as I knew, she'd never had children. "Are you Sally's mother? Is that why you stole her adoption papers? You didn't want her to find out?"

Golda scoffed, but there was a flicker of something in her eyes. "Don't be ridiculous," she said. "Unless you believe in immaculate conception, I can tell you in no uncertain terms that I've never been pregnant, and I've never had a child."

I wished Lily were here with her lie-detector mojo. Even so, it sounded like the truth. "Then what are you hiding?" I pressed. "What promise did you break, and who did you break it with?"

"I should've kept it to myself," she mumbled, suddenly seeming frail beyond her one hundred-plus years. "But I thought I was helping. With Adele gone, I thought she'd be safe."

"Who would be safe?" I leaned forward, though I was sure I had the answer, at least some of it. "Is Sally Adele's daughter?"

Golda blinked, her eyes wild as if looking for an escape. Finally, she nodded. "I wanted to protect her. I swore to Adele that I would never tell. Why, oh why, did I break that promise?"

"Did she steal the records for you?" I shook my head. "Sally has a realty company. She's probably more familiar with the county clerk's office than anyone, except maybe Tyris."

The historian's expression told me I'd hit the nail on the head.

"Adele made me her beneficiary upon her death. I sold what I could anonymously and gave Sally every cent of it. I felt she'd missed out on her birthright because Adele never wanted a child. I watched over her the best I could, but it's not the same as having the birthright and ancestry of a founding witch."

"None of that sounds like a bad thing. What happened after?"

"She wanted to know more about Adele, but

Adele and I had stopped being close decades ago. I'd loved her once, and she'd loved me. It's the reason I kept her secrets. With her estate, I also inherited her diaries," Golda said. "I leafed through them, and there didn't seem to be anything too terrible in them, so I gave them to Sally."

"And then?"

"She discovered a secret text that only revealed itself to someone with Adele's blood." The older witch's eyes were bleak. "After that, Sally grew angry, so very angry." Her gaze pivoted to mine. "She blames you, Hazel. She blames you for Adele's death. I tried to tell her that Adele made terrible, evil choices, that she murdered innocent shifters for the sake of power, but she said her mother spoke to her, and that..."

A door at the back of the house slammed. Golda's lips thinned into a tight line.

"Was that her?" I asked.

The broken woman nodded. "I can't save her, can I?"

I shook my head. "I don't think so, but I'll do my best to bring her in alive." Goddess in a graveyard. Sally Teeter was Adele Abbot's offspring.

"I swear I didn't know, Hazel," she said. "When she told me she saw you kill the werewolf, I knew in my gut that it wasn't true. But I wanted to believe her. She'd been so upset about discovering her true origins. I'd hoped the money would be enough to assuage my guilt, but Sally had been a happy girl before my good intentions. I ruined her."

The pieces were falling into place. Sally had bought Wonderland Realty from Robert Townsend's estate. When the werewolf beta had been dying, he said wonder. What if he'd been trying to say Wonderland? Was sweet Sally Teeter really the mastermind behind all this chaos? Was she capable? The answer was yes, if the apple didn't fall far from the tree. "Do you know where she went or what she has planned?"

Golda shook her head. "I don't know about her plans. She's a more powerful witch now. I could feel it in the same way I'd felt it in Adele. I can guess where she's going, though."

I could guess as well. "The community center. Ford's trial."

She nodded gravely. "If she's responsible for all this, she'll want to see her plot play out."

"To what end?"

"She blames Ford and you for Adele's death. She wants you both to suffer. She wants you to suffer in the same way she feels she has."

I blinked. "In the same way?"

Golda seemed to hear herself as well. "Oh, Goddess." She raised her hand to her mouth. "Kent and Bryant will be at the trial. I'm sure Anita will be there too. She'll want to be there for Ford."

And if Sally killed Jensen and Dick, then she was juiced up on powerful Arete magic. The unstable woman was a time bomb ready to blow. I got up and ran out the door without a word of goodbye. I had to get to the community center. I didn't know what Sally was planning, but I wasn't prepared to become an orphan to find out.

CHAPTER 15

APPARATING TO THE community center had been a risk, but there had been no time to waste. I muttered the spell under my breath, aiming for a discreet location in the building. I prayed to the Goddess that I wouldn't end up in the pool or, worse, a concrete wall. I embraced the magic as it wrapped around me, and I poofed from Golda's yard into the frying pan. Literally.

Yep, when I landed, it wasn't in the shadows or at the back of the room as I'd intended. Nope, I'd translocated right into the center of the stage, the bright lights glaring down on me. I blinked against the sudden brightness, squinting to make out the rows of shocked faces staring up at me. Looking down, I realized I was me again, not Tanya. The translocation spell must've neutralized the illusion magic. Whatever.

I didn't care who saw me at this point. I was here to save my family... or I'd die trying. The gym floor was filled with spectators in chairs, with more crowded into the bleachers. I guess the whole town really had come out for the farce of a trial.

I barely had time to register the gravity of the situation before a massive figure stepped forward. The Beastwarden, a hulking man over seven feet tall with thick orange-blonde hair and a scraggly beard, loomed over me. His arms bulged with veined muscles, and he looked like he could snap me in two without breaking a sweat.

To his right, the three faction alphas—Bryant, Mary, and Steve—sat on folding metal chairs, their eyes fixed on me with varying degrees of surprise and confusion. Ford, the love of my life, sat alone to the Beastwarden's left, bound by ornate, oversized shackles on his wrists and ankles. Most likely magical in origin and designed to keep him from shifting into his bear form.

The front rows were packed with werewolves, with Jensen's second-in-command sitting in the first seat, his eyes narrowed as he watched me. The entire auditorium was a roiling mass of confusion and tension, the shifters in the audience murmuring in disbelief at my sudden appearance.

The Beastwarden recovered first, his voice a deep

rumble as he barked out an order. "Get off the stage, witch!"

I looked him dead in the eye, my heart pounding but my voice steady. "You have no control over me. I'm not a shifter."

The room erupted. Gasps and whispers spread like wildfire through the crowd. The Beastwarden's eyes flared with anger, and for a moment, I thought he might charge at me right then and there.

I didn't back down. I couldn't. Not with Ford chained up like an animal on display, and certainly not with whatever twisted plan Sally Teeter had in store for my dad and Ford's parents. This was my chance to stop her before she could hurt anyone else, and I had to take it.

The Beastwarden, the shifter boogeyman himself, was not someone who tolerated defiance. His eyes narrowed, his massive frame tensing as I stood my ground on the stage. I nearly choked on the tension as the shifters and witches in the auditorium held their collective breath, waiting to see what would happen next.

I glanced to the bottom row of the bleachers and spotted my dad. He sat with Tizzy, my tiny squirrel familiar, perched comfortably in his lap. By his side, his own familiar, Lupitia, a regal gray Persian cat, watched the scene with disinterested eyes. Next to him, Anita Bryant was wringing her hands, her face pale as she awaited her son's fate. But I couldn't focus on her anxiety—not when the real problem was bigger than the trial.

I needed to find Sally Teeter and stop her before she did something I couldn't live with.

I scanned the gym, searching for her. It took me a few seconds, but I spotted her near the doorway at the back of the room. She looked enraged, her eyes hard, and her expression pinched. Without thinking, I lunged forward and snatched the microphone from the Beastwarden's massive hands. His surprised growl echoed through the room. I felt it all the way from the top of my head to the tip of my toes, but I ignored it. Sticks and stones and all that jazz. His growl would not hurt me. However, Sally's unhinged sticks and stones could destroy all of us.

"Sally Teeter!" I shouted, my voice amplified through the speakers. "You're under arrest for the murder of Brahm Jensen and Dick...er, Richard, the beta werewolf. You have the right to remain—"

Before I could finish, a bolt of pure and vicious energy shot from Sally's hands, heading straight for me. I barely had time to react, diving to the side as the beam seared through the air. It missed me by inches and burned a baseball-sized hole through the podium near the Beastwarden. He let out a string of curses, his temper flaring as he hauled Ford off his feet with a single hand and threw him behind the stage, out of harm's way. Bryant, Mary, and Steve scattered, diving for cover as chaos erupted in the gym.

"I think that proves, beyond any doubt, that I'm not the only one who can burn holes through crap!" I said into the microphone, more for the crowd's sake than Sally's. "Stand down," I ordered the rogue witch. "Come in peaceably, and no one else needs to get hurt."

The crowd was in shock, shouts of dismay and fear echoing off the walls. I rolled to my feet just in time to dodge another bolt of energy that crackled through the space where I had just been sitting. The heat from her magic made the air smell like ozone, and I could feel the raw power radiating from Sally, power that had come from the Arete sacrifices.

I had to stop her, but the odds weren't in my favor. Sally was juiced up, fueled by anger and dark magic, and I knew I was in way over my head. Now would've been a perfect time for the Grand Inquisitor to show up with her enforcers and take a bad witch down, but no. My grandmother was nowhere to be seen.

Ack. I had to find a way to end this before Sally took out our entire town in one go.

The gymnasium erupted into chaos as Sally unleashed her wrath. I could feel the crackle of her raw energy in the air, each bolt she fired more powerful than the last. There was no time to think—only time to move. I could hear Ford growling and roaring on the other side of the stage. So I dived in that direction, rolling off the back of the platform and narrowly avoiding another beam of energy that scorched the floor where I'd just been. The impact sent a shockwave through the room, toppling the folding chairs in the front row and sending the first few rows of werewolves scrambling for cover. I crawled to my husband as he struggled to free himself from the cuffs. The Beastwarden was a few feet away, and he had a missing chunk of muscle from his right arm. He'd been hit.

"Unlock the shackles!" I yelled at him.

The stubborn ass shook his head.

"Unlock it or I'll put another hole in you, Beast."

His eyes widened before he finally said, "Cawallah Shumbakay."

The words did the trick as Ford's shackles fell off. "Sally Teeter," he growled. "It was Sally the whole time?"

"I'll explain later," I told him. "Right now, you have to find your mom and both our dads," I told him. "Sally wants to kill them," I added for urgency. "You need to get them to safety."

"What about you?"

"You know me, I'll kick her punk ass from here to Kansas City."

He smirked then kissed me. "You're my badass."

"And you're mine." I kissed him back. "Go get the parents to safety. I'll handle Sally." At least, I hoped I would.

"What about the werewolves?"

"When you get back, those jerks are all yours."

His grin was feral as he hulked out into his half-bear form and roared so loud it shook the rafters. Dayam, my man was freaking sexy.

Oh, Goddess. I realized Tizzy had been right. Danger and chaos were my aphrodisiacs of choice. Yikes. Maybe I was becoming a little too self-aware. A little delusion wasn't a bad thing.

There was another explosion, which meant it was time to get back into the fight.

"Get her!" someone yelled from the bleachers, and suddenly, a barrage of spells launched toward Sally from all directions. The witches and warlocks had combined their efforts to take on the mad realtor.

Lightning crackled through the air, a storm of bright, jagged arcs aimed at Sally from a group of warlocks and witches on the left side of the gym. The force of their combined attack would have brought down an average witch, but super-charged Sally barely flinched. With a wave of her hand, she deflected the lightning bolts, sending them crashing into the ceiling, where they exploded into a shower of sparks.

Another group of witches tried to trap Sally with a binding spell, intricate chains of violet energy weaving through the air toward her. Sally's eyes flashed with fury as she snapped her fingers, and the chains disintegrated mid-air, falling harmlessly to the ground like wisps of smoke. The witch staggered back, her face pale with shock.

Wowza, what had been in Adele's books that had turned Sally into a magic-wielding Terminator?

Officers Parker and Newsome, a warlock and witch, had joined the fight. Their presence bolstered me. I needed to act fast. Drawing on my own magic, I chanted,

"Goddess, help me scratch this itch
I need to beat the little witch,
Send through me a northern wind
The witch to hell it will send
So mote it be."

The spell conjured a blast of icy wind meant to knock Sally off her feet. It whipped through the gym like a hurricane, sending papers flying and knocking over what remained of the podium and the platform that held it. But Sally stood her ground, her feet rooted like an immovable force. She sneered, raising her hands to counter my attack with a gust of her own. The wind met mine head-on, and for a moment, it felt like the whole world was caught in the middle of our struggle. Witches, warlocks, and shifters began running away. I didn't blame them. Nothing we'd used worked on her.

Sally was winning.

Adele's mini-me focused her attention on me as the auditorium cleared out, her eyes blazing with psychotic fury and power. She lifted her hand, gathering energy into a ball of crackling, white-hot light. It was larger than the last several shots, and I knew if that hit me, I wouldn't stand a chance.

Desperation surged through me. I had to think fast and do something that would give me an edge. I reached into the depths of my magic, pulling every last ounce of power I had left. Then, with a cry, I thrust my hands forward, sending a torrent of electricity straight at Sally. But even as it staggered her, I knew it wouldn't be enough. Sally screamed in anger, not pain, as she shook off my magic. Her expression twisted, making her look even more maniacal. She raised her hands again, and this time, the energy that formed between them was inky black and swirling with malevolent power. She was about to unleash something devastating enough to wipe out everyone left in this room, including me.

The Beastwarden, who had been injured on the sidelines, decided to jump into the fray. With a bellowing roar, he charged Sally, his massive form towering over her. He moved faster than I expected, his colossal hand reaching out to crush the rogue witch's skull with the full force of a shifter's strength.

But Sally was quicker. She twisted out of his grasp, her dark energy blasting the Beastwarden in the chest and sending him hurtling across the stage. He crashed into the wall with a deafening thud, the impact cracking the cinder blocks and sending dust and debris cascading to the floor.

Once again, she turned back to me, her eyes alight with the thrill of battle. She had gone too far, and I knew she wouldn't stop until she'd destroyed everything in her path. I came to the realization that I couldn't beat her. Her magic was too powerful, but it didn't mean I would give up. I'd taken an oath to protect the people in this town, and I would fulfill my oath to my dying breath.

With no other choice, I braced myself for her next attack, knowing that this might be my last stand. But even as fear gnawed at me, I would give everything I had, even to my last breath.

Sally raised her hands one final time, the dark energy swirling in her palms, ready to strike. And I knew this was it—the moment that would decide everything.

"Hazel!" I heard Tizzy scream. I looked up to see my flying squirrel gliding through the air. She had something large in her back claws, and she let it drop when she was passing over my head. "Catch!"

Like a rock, my 9mm weapon fell into my hands. My confusion lasted all of one second before I acted. I raised my hand at the same time that Sally let loose her terrifying magic, and I shot her through the forehead. The magic hit me, and I screamed as it burned into my side, but as Sally dropped lifeless to the gym floor, the dark magic died with her. I sagged, falling to my knees as the fight left my body.

Tizzy ran to me. "Hazel!" She climbed my shirt and put her face against mine. "You're alive. I can't believe it. I thought for sure that witch had you."

"Me too," I said numbly, somewhat unable to believe I was still alive. I felt no remorse for ending her. It was her or me and the rest of the town. The decision had been easy. "Thanks, Tiz. Thanks for knowing what I needed."

"Aw-shucks." Tiz brushed my face with her whiskers. "Magic wasn't cutting it, so I figured some good old-fashioned hot lead and steel might do the trick."

I nodded at Sally's lifeless body. "Sure did."

CHAPTER 16

TANYA GELLAR TROTTED across the gym with her medical bag once my officers gave her the all-clear. "Let me check you over."

"I'm okay." I gave her a heartfelt hug first before shooing her away. She'd come through for me big time, and I would never forget it. "Go help the others." I gestured to the Beastwarden. "He's got a big chunk missing from his arm."

Ford rushed over, still slightly furred. Tizzy moved out of the get-squished path as he hugged me tightly. "Are you okay?"

"I'm okay. A little bruised and exhausted, but I'm not broken."

"I knew you had it," he whispered against my hair.

"The parents?" I asked.

"All safe," he said. He glanced at Sally. "A magic bullet?"

"Opposite," I told him. "She was immune to all magic. It was something mundane that finally took her down." I was sorry I'd been forced to kill her, but if I hadn't, she wouldn't have stopped her rampage of torture and death. "Can we go home?"

"Not yet," the Beastwarden barked. "This doesn't change the fact that a charge has been levied against Ford Baylor, and that has to be addressed."

"Right," Ardell, Jensen's second, shouted from high up in the bleachers. He and a few of his werewolves had hidden up there during the fight. Cowards. "This territory is now ours. We want our due."

"You've got to be kidding me?" I groaned. "I think it's obvious that neither Ford nor I had anything to do with Jensen's death. Henceforth and so on, he's innocent."

"It doesn't change the situation," he said with a guttural rasp. The idiot was obviously in pain. I guess it was true—misery loves company.

"You're not taking my husband." I waggled the end of my gun in his general direction. "Unless you want me to shoot you too."

Ford put his arms around me again. "No one is shooting anyone."

"Because it won't be necessary," the Grand

Inquisitor announced from the open doors. "I've found the proof!" She had my cell phone in her hand and walked it over to the Beastwarden.

"What's this?" he asked.

"I like 'em big and dumb in bed," my grandmother said, "but not at work. Wise up. It's a text message from one of Brahm Jensen's own men telling Hazel to meet him at the park. The timestamp is after the time of death."

"The number is from an unknown caller. It's not proof." The Beastwarden seemed less gung-ho now. Clementine Battles had a way of taking the wind out of someone's sails.

"You want proof?" She gestured to me. "Hazel, do your thing."

"My thing?" The magic fight must've mushed my brain because I had no idea what she was talking about. "What thing?"

She bobbled her head back and forth. "Your reveal spell thing."

"Oh." Duh. She handed me my phone, and I concentrated on the "Unknown" part of the text.

"Goddess, bring me second sight.

Turn the darkness into light.

What once was unknown, let it be shown.

Reveal a path, make the unseen seen.

Done and done, Goddess grant to me,

Second sight, so mote it be."

The word "Unknown" began to glow for me as the letters turned and twisted and became a set of numbers.

"What's happening?" the Beastwarden asked, not able to see the numbers that were revealed to me.

"Just watch," my grandmother told him.

I punched in the sequence of numbers, and a phone at the top of the bleachers began to ring. I noticed the second in command, who was not the alpha with Jensen out of the way, looked really uncomfortable.

The Beastwarden glared at the werewolf. "Pick it up," he demanded.

Instead, Ardell shot up from the bench and took off running across the bleachers toward the door.

"He's getting away," I told the Beastwarden.

"Not for long," he replied in a steely tone that sent shivers up my spine. "Trial is over. Ford Baylor is not guilty. The werewolf pack will vacate Merry County, and when I get Ardell Singer, he'll pay for his crime." The enormous man nodded to my grandmother. "Grand Inquisitor," he said. "Ever the pleasure."

She smiled. "Same, Beastwarden. Same."

Ford and I exchanged looks as we witnessed the chemistry between two extremely powerful creatures. Honestly, it scared me a little.

"Can we go home?" I asked again.

"What she said," Tizzy added. I noticed she was watching forlornly as Lupitia walked off with a ginger and white cat. "I don't want to be here anymore."

"I'm sorry, Tiz." I cuddled her close to me. "This really sucks."

"Go home," Grandmother said. "I'll come over later to see you before I leave."

Ford helped me to my feet, and we walked out of the building together. I saw my father and Ford's parents in the parking lot. I had known Ford would keep them safe, but I still breathed a sigh of relief.

"Tizzy!" Lupitia shouted. "Wait up."

"Keep walking," Tiz said as she snuggled closer. "I don't want to see her right now. She can break up with me tomorrow."

"Tisiphone!" the cat cried out. "Wait."

Tizzy skittered up my shirt and climbed onto my shoulder. "If you wanted to break up with me, you should've just told me. You didn't have to cheat on me."

"What are you talking about?" the Persian asked, bewildered. "Who cheated?"

"You!" She pointed a tiny claw at the cat. "I saw you." She pointed to Spike. "With him two nights ago right here in this parking lot."

Lupitia let out a string of expletives that would curl a sailor's toes. "I'm not cheating on you."

"Well, you sure as heck aren't going to Book Club."

"No, you're right. I haven't been going to Book Club. I've been in rehearsal!"

"For?" Tizzy demanded, wildly confused.

"You!" Lupita announced with a cat that ate the canary grin.

This was getting long, messy, and weird, and the only long and messy I wanted was the six-foot-five bear trying to take me to bed. I could do without the weird all together. "Can you two talk at home?"

"No," Lupitia said again, but with more vigor. "Because I have something I want to say to Tisiphone. I want her to know that I've had the time of my life."

Music began to play. It was the song from *Dirty Dancing*.

I looked back to see Lupitia swaying and swishing as she strutted toward us. She lip-synced to the song as several other familiars joined the dance.

I looked at Ford. "What is happening?"

"I don't honestly know," he said, "but it's freaking me out."

"It's a flash mob," someone yelled. "Aren't they adorable?"

What an afternoon. We'd gone from shrieking and running for our lives to adorable dancing animals. More proof that the paranormal community was a resilient bunch—albeit crazy.

When the song moved into the bridge, Lupitia stood up on her hind legs and held out a paw. "No one puts Tizzy in the corner," she announced.

Tizzy jumped down from my shoulder and took Lupitia's paw.

I wasn't sure if it was going to happen, but sure enough, Lupitia danced away from Tiz and then held out her front legs. Magnificently, my happy familiar took off at a run and flung herself in the air, landing less than gracefully on top of her Persian girlfriend. This knocked her over, and they both rolled off the sidewalk into the grass. The growing crowd went wild with applause. When the two cute critters got up and dusted the grass off, Lupitia asked, "Tisiphone, as the song says, I've never felt this way before, and it's all because of you. Would you do me the greatest honor by consenting to be my wife?"

Unexpectedly, a sob choked from my throat when Tiz shouted, "Yes!" Of course, then she turned on me and said, "See, Hazel, I told you she wasn't cheating on me."

I rolled my teary eyes and laughed. "Congratulations, Tiz, I'm so happy for you." I sagged against Ford's arms. "Can you take me home now?"

"Yes, love." He wrapped me in his warm embrace. "There's no place I'd rather be."

A week later, my grandmother confirmed what I'd suspected about Sally. The innocent-looking diaries had been spelled by Adele, and the secrets they revealed to Sally had driven her mad. There were contacts in the books for other groups of Arete. It's how Sally had found Brahm Jensen. The Beastwarden had gotten a full confession out of Ardell. Ardell didn't make it out of the interrogation alive. The Beastwarden didn't suffer fools or criminals lightly.

Sally had stolen the real deed to Clayton Driver's property and used her know-how as a realtor to forge a new one. Only, when Jensen arrived, Sally figured out fast that she couldn't control the strong alpha, so she plotted with his second to steal his power and blame it all on Ford and me. She'd wanted us out, but she hadn't wanted Jensen to have any real control over our town. She'd also been the one to grow the tree where they sacrificed Dick. She clearly had the same gift as Pierce. It made me wonder if Pierce hated me so much because he'd once been Adele's lover. Maybe even the father of the child she never wanted. It was better not to speculate. I didn't need another person from that family forming a vendetta against me and mine.

Ford and I were planning a vacation—a real one with views, drinks, and room service. Tiz and Lupitia were planning a wedding. I loved my family, and they loved me, and once again, my boring little town was boring again. And that was just fine by me. Never again would I complain about being bored...who was I kidding? I was already itching for our next adventure, and with Ford by my side there was nothing we couldn't tackle.

The End...for now

BURNING DJINN OF FIRE – SNEAK PEEK

Seven months ago, goddess magic allowed me, the very human Marigold Everlee, to have a couple of sizzling nights with the very paranormal Zev. He was tall, dark, and smoking hot.

Literally. He's an ifrit--a fire-magic-wielding djinn.

Spoiler alert: When the goddess magic poofed---so did Zev.

Yeah. I was ghosted after he promised me, he'd be back. His disappearance turned my heart to ash. But you know what? I'm middle-aged and marvelous, baby. Crying over spilled magic isn't going to change what happened to my one-sided love connection.

I have new aspirations: being the best bad-ass witch possible. My new bestie is teaching me the ways of eclectic magic, and I'm throwing all my energy into the process. I've always been a little hippy-dippy, so using my crystals and herbs for spell work should come naturally to me, right?

Wrong.

Just when I think I'm getting the hang of potions, a fire spell blows up in my face, leaving a cryptic message scorched into my kitchen ceiling.

From Zev. *What the what!?*

It seems Zev didn't want to disappear after all.

I may be a magical mess, but no one gets away with hurting the people I love, including my stubborn, sarcastic, sexy genie.

Watch out, world. This girl is on fire. Get out of the way ... or get burned.

Chapter One

Seven months earlier...

The acrid stench of the giant, horrid beast turned my stomach. With a name like snotgurgle, I knew it would be disgusting, but I hadn't been prepared for how much nauseating mucus would be covering the creature. It resembled a colossal green booger. So freaking gross.

"Oh, holy monstrosity." I swallowed as the sour taste of bile filled my mouth. I watched Zev, an annoyingly charming and unholy handsome fire djinn, run across the expansive field with the snotgurgle hot on his heels.

My heart skipped a beat. I wanted to yell at him to get his ifrit ass moving, but obviously, he was booking as fast as he could.

I hadn't seen him since the pixie mating frenzy until today, but man, I thought about him a lot. He'd shown up at the Iron Grove earlier that day. Keir had called him to act as Iris's fire guardian for her witch trial.

It was as bad as it sounded.

As the beast closed in on Zev, I staggered forward.

"Don't expose yourself, Marigold," Carver Martin, an eclectic witch I'd only met hours earlier, warned as he tugged me down, shielding me with the stone barrier outside the hedge maze behind the Iron Grove. "You don't want him catching your scent. Snotgurgles are relentless once they start hunting. Besides, you get slimed, you get dead."

Carver's father, Thomas, the witch of Archdruid Freya, had assigned Carver the task of babysitting me. Honestly, I thought it was Thomas' way of keeping both of us out of harm. A part of me felt like I was responsible for what was happening. My sister's boyfriend and magical mentor, Keir, had asked me to bring Iris her grimoires, and I'd asked Linda the Gnome to come along for the ride.

How in the hell could I have known that gnomes were a delicacy for Snotgurgles? Oh, and guess what else? Snotgurgles were nasty trolls that took great delight in torturing their food before eating it. I hoped like hell it hadn't eaten Linda.

I'd never forgive myself.

My anxiety level ramped up to ten as I gnawed on my thumbnail. Ugh. I'd already chewed all my fingernails until they bled. I dropped my hand and turned my gaze to Carver. "We can't hide. We have to help."

"How do you suggest we help?" Carver asked. His unnaturally black hair had fallen over his bushy brows and into his eyes. He brushed it back. "The druids and their tru-craft witches will struggle to take that creature down. This kind of troll is immune to magic and most physical attacks. His mucous is poisonous, and the snot from its nose can dissolve flesh and bone. You go out there, and they'll have to worry about protecting you while trying to do an already impossible job."

"Fine," I conceded. Carver and his stupid logic. "I can't believe creatures like this exist." It was a sentiment I'd repeated to myself often since finding out my sister Iris was a tru-craft witch.

"I wish the snotgurgle was the worst thing I've ever seen," Carver muttered.

I didn't have the emotional capacity to think about what could be worse. My fears were for the people I loved. "What about my sister?" I craned my neck again to see if I could spot her on the field. Zev had come out of the woods with the monster, but I hadn't seen Iris. "Where is she?"

Carver put his hand on my shoulder and gave it a gentle squeeze. "Iris is strong, and so is Keir. Keep the faith."

Easier said than done. I'd never been religious, but I'd always been drawn to the spirituality of the natural world, so I prayed to anyone who might be listening to keep my sister and Keir safe. And Zev, too.

The archdruids and their witches lined up on the grassy field like a small army, ready to do battle against the monstrous abomination.

"I hope you're right." I couldn't cower away. People I cared about—that I loved—were in danger, and I'd never been one to sit on the sidelines. Hell, I was usually the person starting the fight. Hiding behind a wall wasn't my jam.

I moved again for a better look, shrugging Carver's hand off when he attempted to stop me.

The snotgurgle, less than impressed by his newfound foes, undulated his gelatinous body in a horrifying dance. His gyrating bulbous hips shot fluorescent green globs of slime that sprayed over the grass and foliage.

I blinked. "Is that grass turning black?" The area around the snotgurgle had turned into a giant inky shadow surrounding the creature.

"Everything the slime touches dies," Carver said. "If I could find a vessel to collect some, I could formulate a spell or potion to neutralize the effects."

I whipped my gaze to him. "Can you do that now?"

He shook his head solemnly. "No. It would take hours, maybe days, to craft the right combination." His fists clenched as he rubbed his knuckles against the side of his black jeans. "I hate being sidelined."

I arched my brow. He'd argued with me about following the archdruids to the field, but I wondered if it was an argument he'd had no intention of winning. "You're worried, too. About your dad?"

"Thomas isn't my dad," he said without anger or malice. "He's my friend. And yes, I'm worried about him."

Biologically, Thomas was his father, but like me, Carver had been adopted as a baby and raised by parents who had loved him well. My dad was my dad, and no amount of genetics or lack thereof would change that fact. The same seemed to be true for Carver.

I nodded. "Thomas is powerful, too, and from what Iris has said, he's fought and survived other battles. They'll win," I told him with far more confidence than I felt. "They have to." I gasped, my relief palpable, when my sister Iris and Keir burst out of the forest at a full sprint. "Oh, thank everything good and chocolatey," I whispered.

Keir raced ahead of Iris, both of them looking as if they'd been run through the spin cycle before coming to an abrupt halt. The snotgurgle was caught between them and the archdruids.

Freya stood with Thomas and the others, each with a man or a woman by their side, hands joined.

"Power of air," I heard Thomas call out. "I bind thee to mine and thine, my kin to call and summon. Obey my will."

"Power of fire," a tall brunette with straight dark hair said, "I bind thee to mine and thine, my kin to call and summon. Obey my will."

A curvy woman wearing a bright red rockabilly dress covered in white polka dots shouted, "Power of earth. I bind thee to mine and thine, my kin to call and summon. Obey my will."

"Why isn't anything happening?" I demanded of Carver.

"Just wait," he answered without looking at me. His eyes were glued to the action... or rather lack thereof. "They're not done."

A petite blonde in a long white maxi dress voiced clearly, "Power of water, I bind thee to mine and thine, my kin to call and summon. Obey my will."

That was four elements from four out of the six druid groves.

Another woman with dark hair intoned, "Power of Air, I bind thee to mine and thine, my kin to call and summon. Obey my will."

That left only the Bezoar Grove to join in, and I wondered if Mathias Easton, the Ichabod Crane-looking leader of the grove, would allow old scars to see this assault on Iron Grove as an opportunity.

Easton's coven leader, a guy who was just as skinny and tall as he was, hesitated only a moment before adding his own command, "Power of Fire, I bind thee to mine and thine, my kin to call and summon. Obey my will."

Why wasn't anything happening? The snotgurgle had stopped his death dance and scratched his head as he stared at the group of druids and witches.

A sonic boom struck the center of the field.

Carver and I were slammed to the ground. I scrambled to my feet to watch the horror unfold as glowing mucus exploded from the snotgurgle, followed by shouts of alarm.

The giant troll roared as it threw back his head and sneezed, sending the largest loogie I've ever seen toward Archdruid Freya. Carver lurched forward, and then I watched helplessly as Zev jumped in front of Freya to take the hit.

A scream of anguish ripped my throat as I watched him crumple to the ground. "Zev!" Without thinking, I hiked up my skirt and sprinted toward the fallen ifrit.

I heard other roars, shouts, and screams, but I couldn't focus on them. I had to get to Zev. He hadn't moved since the rotting slime had hit him in the chest.

Let him be alive, I prayed. Don't let him die. I'd been flirting with the fiery ifrit for only a couple of months, but as the possibility of losing him forever loomed, I realized that my feelings for him went beyond a crush. He was a creature of fire, and I was a human. We couldn't be together. He'd told me that from the start, but the reality hadn't stopped my heart from opening and letting him in.

People were going down around me, but I was almost there. Twenty more yards. I can make it, I told myself. I high-stepped around several piles of goo. I was almost there!

I heard Iris's voice shouting above the fray, but I couldn't worry about what she was doing. Zev had risked his life to save everyone, and no one was trying to save him.

"Zev," I yelled as I slid to a halt and dropped to the ground beside him. The slime had burned through his leather jacket and was eating a hole into his chest. Flames swirled inside the wounds.

He turned to look at me, his eyes wide and his face a picture of pain. "No, *libbu ša*, you cannot be here," he managed to say. "Run, my beautiful love. Run."

"No," I told him. "I'm not leaving without you." I grabbed his arm to drag him away from the fight, and the skin on my hands and arms began to blister.

He yanked his body away, muttering in a language I couldn't understand, but it didn't stop me from getting the gist. He didn't want me to touch him. "I can't control the fire," he said. "You can't help me. You must go.'

Scalding tears burned my eyes. "I won't. I won't leave you."

A burst of colorful lights lit the night sky. I glanced away from Zev to see my sister floating in the air. Numbly, I asked, "What is she doing?"

My question was sort of answered when she

bellowed, "I am Macha, earth mother and destroyer of men. You will come to heel!"

Who in the world was Macha? Had everyone lost their damned minds? Witches and most of the druids dropped to the ground as her light washed over the battlefield. The snotgurgle bellowed, beating his chest. His slimy coating grew even thicker over his skin.

My sister chanted some jibber-jabber words that I didn't understand. "Addlebyörn Bulbusbilgerbiersven of Höga Kusten."

But the troll responded with his own string of garbled words. "Du vet mitt namn?"

It shot a hot glob at her, and I shuddered as she swiped it away as if she were shooing a fly. "You cannot defeat me, creature," she told it. "I am your undoing."

I felt a cold slap of putrid droplets as the snotgurgle shook his body like a dog after a bath. Searing pain burrowed into my side, and the left side of my face felt as if it were on fire. I looked down at Zev, my mouth open to scream, but I couldn't breathe, let alone make a sound.

"Marigold," he rasped.

"Iris!" someone near me yelled.

I collapsed to the ground, sucking to take in air. It must've taken all his will, and maybe some magic, but Zev managed to crawl to me. He wrapped me in his arms, his heated embrace a welcome respite to the cold chill consuming me. Flaming tears rolled down his cheeks as he cradled me in his lap.

"Don't try to move," he said when I reached up to touch his face. "Save your strength."

I mouthed, "We are together."

His eyes burned blue with the brightest flame. "Hush, my darling."

"We can't save what she is," I heard Iris say, but her voice sounded different. "There is a cost...."

Was Zev getting less hot, or was death finally taking me?

"We're losing her!" Keir shouted. "Iris! The rot is making it impossible to heal her. We can't stop it. Every time Zev tries, it takes more from her and more from him. It's like it's feeding on the magic, and they're both dying."

"I will fix the woman, as you say, Iris Everlee," Iris said. "Olwen, who faced thirteen harrowing trials to win the heart of her love, your line runs true in this one. She is strong, a warrior's heart." Her hands glowed as she touched my forehead. "Transform, daughter," she commanded. "Transform and live."

I drew in a welcome breath as the agony disappeared. I could feel my muscles and bones shifting beneath my skin, and I blinked at Zev.

He let out a heaving sigh and then let me go as

he fell over. Whatever was happening in my body made it impossible to move, speak, or help.

I tensed as Iris touched Zev's face. "Your time is not over, Za'fir of Mesopotamia. This is just the first trial on your path to love." Her hand glowed again and Zev's entire body bathed in her light. "Transform and live. Live to fulfill your path."

I let out a sob as Zev's cavernous chest wound knitted together, and his eyes opened. Flames shot out of his mouth and into the sky. When the stream of fire subsided, he collapsed back and passed out.

"Marigold," I heard Iris say as the world turned blissfully floaty. "What's wrong with her?"

"It's probably a side effect of Macha's magic," Keir replied. "She'll be okay. Zev, too."

As I awakened, my head swam with momentary confusion, and then I remembered. Zev had cried as he'd held me in his arms. He'd been in rough shape —we both had—but Iris had healed us. I squinted as I opened my eyes. "Zev?"

"I am here." His rich amber-brown eyes were framed by thick, dark lashes as his gaze met mine.

I was lying on a narrow mattress, and the small area around us was encircled by a white curtain. "Where are we?"

"The ballroom has been turned into a medical ward," he replied.

I frowned. There was something different about him. It wasn't the lustrous dark brown hair full of loose curls that made me want to run my fingers through them or his olive-tone skin, high cheekbones, and sharp jawline that made me want to take up sculpting.

"Zev," I said, my voice barely above a whisper as I studied him, the familiar leather jacket draped over his shoulder as he stood there.

"Marigold," he replied, his voice a low, rumbling murmur that sent a jolt of electricity coursing through me. "I feared I'd lost you forever."

I reached out, my fingers trembling as they brushed against his hand, feeling the warmth of his skin beneath my touch. Only, he was less warm than usual. Strange.

"Zev," I murmured, my heart pounding in my chest. "Are you ... are you okay? Why in the world did you jump in front of that nuclear snot rocket?"

"I owed Freya," he replied. With his other hand, he turned a flat circular stone across his knuckles like a coin. He flipped his hand over, and the stone was nestled in his hand. "My debt has been paid." He pressed the stone into my palm. It was smooth, shiny, and black with red veins. Etched in the top were a series of pointy triangles going in many directions.

"What's this?"

"It's *sebtusiptu*." Zev smiled. "A token."

The stone felt warm against my skin, and the longer I held it, the warmer it got. "A token for what?"

His brow raised as his smile turned sly. He closed my fingers around the token until my hand was a fist, and then he raised my knuckles to his lips and kissed them.

I shivered at the brush of his mouth against my skin. "A token of my esteem."

An unholy, schoolgirl giggle tittered from my lips. Ugh. How embarrassing.

His eyes, that's what was different. "Where are your flames?"

"They're no more," he answered quietly. "The goddess Macha has removed my fire."

I tried to punch down the hope surging inside me. "For good?" I sat up and slung my legs over the side of the gurney. Without his flames, we could be together. Was it really possible?

"For now," he replied.

My legs felt strange as they dangled off the edge like they weren't my own. Then I stood up. My brow furrowed. "Did taking your fire make you shorter?"

At five-eight, I was a tall woman, but Zev had been a few inches taller than me. Now, I towered over him.

The corners of his mouth tugged into a smile. "You have also been changed by Macha."

There was a mirror on the wall behind him. I studied my reflection. My straight, dark brown, almost black hair hung loose around my shoulders. My skin had the same kiss of honey that it always did, and my brown eyes hadn't changed colors. Iris used to tell me that I looked like Catherine Zeta-Jones. Other than our coloring, I didn't really see it. "How have I been changed?"

Zev chuckled. "You've grown five inches for one."

"No." I shook my head and scoffed. "That's not a real thing." I looked at my hands. "Where are my rings?"

He gestured to a small side table. A chewed-up mess of metal and stones that vaguely resembled my rings littered a metal tray.

My eyes went wide. "What the hell happened to my jewelry?"

"You grew too big for them. The metal was cutting off the blood supply. It was the rings or your fingers."

My eyes narrowed to slits. "Are you saying I have fat fingers?"

"You have lovely, long fingers, *Libbu ša*, and I would drip them in jewels if that were your wish."

"So, you're granting wishes now, huh? I thought you said genies didn't do that kind of thing."

"I would make an exception for you, my beautiful flower." His dark gaze met mine, and I shivered. "For you, I would grant your every heart's desire."

"Oh, darling, I have a whole laundry list of requests," I smirked. "The first one involves you getting naked."

His grin grew wide. "Naked?"

"In the extreme," I said.

I laughed when he instantly dropped his jacket onto the floor. I set the stone down, and Zev paused his striptease. He picked up the stone and put it with my rings. "This is yours now. Keep it close to you."

I gave him a crooked smile. "As a token of your esteem."

"So a part of me will always be with you."

Present day…

A part of me will always be with you.... Zev's words lingered in my head as I looked around the room, orienting myself back to the present. The walls were covered in macrame art, boho chic straw plates and jars of crystals littering the freestanding shelves. In other words, I was in my own bedroom and no longer at Iron Grove with the fireless ifrit who had metaphorically scorched my panties off.

Even though it had been seven months ago, it felt like yesterday.

I sat up and stretched my back. "Big day," I reminded myself as I picked up Zev's token from the selenite bowl on my nightstand. Holding on to a rock from an ex-lover was silly, but it was tangible evidence that our relationship had been real. It had meant something, and I wasn't ready to give it up. I'd laid my clothes out the night before. A chocolate-tiered maxi skirt with pockets, a yellow and blue floral peasant blouse, and a tan bra and panty set that I loved so much I'd bought them in all the colors. I grabbed up the garments and trekked down the hall to the bathroom.

Carver and the boys would be here soon for our magic lessons and to help me stir a complicated potion—with a few modifications I'd read about on an internet forum for witches. Should I tell him? Probably. Would he try to stop me? Definitely. Which meant I wasn't going to loop him in.

I'd lost Zev, and I worried I'd never get him back.

Not if I didn't take matters into my own hands.

Get Burning Djinn of Fire today!

PARANORMAL MYSTERIES & ROMANCES
BY RENEE GEORGE

Witchin' Impossible Paranormal Mysteries

Witchin' Impossible (Book 1)

Rogue Coven (Book 2)

Familiar Protocol (Booke 3)

Mr & Mrs. Shift (Book 4)

FurOut (Book 5)

Barkside of the Moon Paranormal Mysteries

Pit Perfect Murder (Book 1)

Murder & The Money Pit (Book 2)

The Pit List Murders (Book 3)

Pit & Miss Murder (Book 4)

The Prune Pit Murder (Book 5)

Two Pits and A Little Murder (Book 6)

Pits and Pieces of Murder (Book 7)

Pittie Party Murder (Book 8)

Peculiar Mysteries & Romances

You've Got Tail (Book 1)

My Furry Valentine (Book 2)

Thank You For Not Shifting (Book 3)

My Hairy Halloween (Book 4)

In the Midnight Howl (Book 5)

Furred Lines (Book 6)

My Wolfy Wedding (Book 7)

Who Let The Wolves Out? (Book 8)

My Thanksgiving Faux Paw (Book 9)

Grimoires of a Middle-aged Witch

Earth Spells Are Easy (Book 1)

Spell On Fire (Book 2)

When the Spells Blows (Book 3)

Spell Over Troubled Water (Book 4)

Ghost in the Spell (Book 5)

Destiny of a Middle-aged Witch

Burning Djinn of Fire (Book 1)

Djinn Bottle Blues (Book 2)

Stand By Your Djinn (Book 3)

Nora Black Midlife Psychic Mysteries

Sense & Scent Ability (Book 1)

For Whom the Smell Tolls (Book 2)

War of the Noses (Book 3)

Aroma With A View (Book 4)

Spice and Prejudice (Book 5)

Age of Inno-Scents (Book 6)

Aroma Holiday (Book 7)

Vapes of Wrath (Book 8)

The Scented Cipher (Book 9)

Of Spice and Men (Book 10)

Hex Drive

Hex Me, Baby, One More Time (Book 1)

Oops, I Hexed It Again (Book 2)

I Want Your Hex (Book 3)

Hex Me With Your Best Shot (Book 4)

Hex Me All Night Long (Book 5)

ABOUT THE AUTHOR

USA Today Bestselling Author, Renee George writes paranormal mysteries and romances because she loves all things whodunit, Other-worldly, and weird. Also, she wishes her pittie, the adorable Kona, could talk. Or at least be more like Scooby-Doo and help her unmask villains at the haunted house up the street.

When she's not writing about mystery-solving

werecougars or the adventures of a hapless psychic living among shapeshifters, she dons her superhero cape and rescues kittens. Okay, the kitten totally showed up one day and suddenly she's got a new pet named Simon.

She lives in Missouri with her family and spends her non-writing time doing really cool stuff...like watching TV and cleaning up dog poop.

Join My Newsletter

Follow Me On Bookbub!

Join Renee's Rebel Readers on Facebook!